OGALLALAH De ORO
MY LIFE WITH HUMANS

Twintreess

1996
TreeHouse Press
Tucson, Arizona

Thank you for opening this book.
Please come in.

TreeHouse Press
5738 E. Holmes St. Tucson, AZ 85711 USA
1-800-585-9389

This book is created from our own hands, with a chorus of etheric and physical supporters. Why? We sometimes wondered that ourselves. As timeless beings, we felt that it was sacred to infuse our intent in every step of the book creation process. Co-creating this book is a slice of life. It is all a process, and we bless all the struggles, challenges and unknown miracles still waiting to be discovered.

Copyright 1996 Twintreess

All rights reserved. Any reproduction of any part of this book is possible with written permission from the authors. Please ask us. We want this information to be lovingly shared with all the world and beyond.

Cover artwork by Francene Hart © 1996

First edition.
Printed in the United States of America
Library of Congress Card Catalog Number 96-090335

ISBN # 0-9645194-3-7

Preface

Hi! We are Thomas and Marilyn Twintreess, we thought that you humans might want to connect with some other humans before you venture on this wild, animal, other-worldly journey ... Welcome.

Ogallalah is many things to many people. We all have our own special first meetings with her. For Thomas, she was a teeny puppy, who even then was wild, free and powerful. For Marilyn, she was incredibly beautiful, and perfectly graceful.

Ogallalah is a malamute dog (usually). She is our family. Every decision, every thought, every feeling we have, touches her. We consider her in all things.

Every day, we, Twintreess, consider and

listen to all sorts of life forms. We talk to stones, stars, lakes – actually, everything that wishes to speak to us. Then we record it and share it with all, including humans, and the story of life just grows and grows.

The being who spoke to us least of all, was Ogallalah. We didn't really know why, but maybe we didn't need to know that. Maybe it was enough that she *lived* her words and her ways with us each day. Her every move was a whole language if you listened with your whole heart. We love her any way that she is.

Lately, she has been moving slower and she has had to adjust to our moving to a mountain. Then it happened. "I want to tell you my story," she said, "I will give it to you and you will give it to others."

This is it, just as it happened, day by day. These are her words and we love them all. She inspires us beyond ourselves; we could not have imagined this by ourselves. Thank you, Ogallalah. We deeply honor all that you are, and we will share it with as many people as possible.

Here are her words. They stand alone. You must choose for yourself what your first meeting with Ogallalah will be, as well as all the rest.

One

I could feel it coming. Then, I saw it. An arm of sunlight came from the sky. It sharpened and grew as it traveled before me. I knew it. There was no way to move from it. That clear light would find me and know my heart finally, finally, finally.

I barked.

I said to him, "It's coming, it's coming for me."

In his eyes I couldn't see any reflection of the growing light so I ran around the grass. I made the circle of completion ready. I ran through my life. Then it hit. My heart exploded. At once it was in my chest, next, it fragmented to the universe. I was gone in a million directions at once. Uncounted colors swirled around me. They blinked at my newness and smiled and shaped new hues.

A long, thin, blue line reached me. He said, "Wait. Please don't go yet. Just come back once more!"

6   Ogallalah de Oro

I howled into the sun. All the colors descended into one white ray. I found my heart. I grabbed it. Not for me. I gave it to him.

With my eyes in my heart, I saw his hand touch it. For that moment, I remembered time. I remembered my running body, now dropped onto the earth. I saw the white light in the tips of his fingers. It joined with the ray that was my heart.

Sound came from the light. My heart in his hand pulsed. I recorded this forever because it was my way of telling him that we would always be forever.

Then the rhythm of this new, re-created heartbeat exploded and cast me out to the next freedom. It was my time. There was and is no questioning of that. I carried myself into the sun. When it would be our time, we would remember it all without skipping a beat.

His name is Thomas. I was called Hannah. It is quite intense for me to speak this. As I give you my soul to read, the spirits will show you why.

Thomas and I were a bright couple. Love made us strong. It talked over differences and crept out of every sameness we could find. He walks in the world as a human. I walked on the earth as dog. Sometimes. (You, who cannot see me now, I cry for this bond. I cry to speak of it because it is so holy that I have never thought to give it words. It simply is. Though my body has passed on into a new miracle, this love has easily carried through that transformation. It sees through me to my soul and I cannot hide, in any skin, from it. I tell you this now so your heart will ease into this story even at moments like this when I am stretched taut and halting.)

Welcome to my little story. It grows bigger

because I am different from you listening (and still you can pluck out the sameness). Though I am part dog you recognize me. I know you are weeping in a silent place of you, just as I am. You see, the story of Thomas and me has grown into your story, too. Some day I pray you will give it to another.

In the beginning, I gave you the death of Hannah. For me, it was recorded happily. I left with all life and freedom and I return now for love. Just one more time. Within all that life, that moment lived with me an eternity. It is the mark of passage on my body and I hold it in my breast every second. Each time I feel it, it grows. Though I left that body and I died, I was reborn into Thomas' life forever by love.

Do you find it strange that I can tell you this? Do you wonder what imagination creates me? Well, then, say it aloud. I am honestly being me with you. I ask for the same. Lay all your questions and your answers here. Let me share with you all that I am. When we are done with that road you can come by here and pick up your questions and answers again if you still want them ... if you can still travel the same way back.

What speaks to you now is my complete essence. That is how I can shape any word and give it to you so that you can hope to understand. I am a dog. I feel. I know. I have consciousness to give to any who wishes to receive it. Of course, I have a heart. I am mostly heart.

My Hannah body was buried and my grave was washed in tears. I did not watch this from the sun, but I came to know of this and even seemed to remember it later on. Thomas went on. He walked. He ate. He grew quiet. And he always remembered that a piece of his heart had traveled on. I loved that.

I have been taught different kinds of spirit travel by humans and creatures and the invisible ones. So I

8   Ogallalah de Oro

visited Thomas by night. With all my being I gave him my secret name. I let him see me in my power. Every light showed me and I stepped from inside of them into his dream heart. He saw me. He saw my soul. For him, it came onto him as a beautiful woman. I was robed all in white and had long braids. My spirit sang the songs of the ancient shamans. I held his hand and there were no paws or fur between us. It was all the beauty that we could imagine together at once.

We walked through the woods. He stared at me and said, "Who are you?" I smiled. I pointed to the trees and I knew that he would make whatever meaning he could. Silently, I told him that the trees would always answer all his needs and that his name was inscribed upon their essence.

Did he hear me? No. As is right by spirit and truth, he heard my laughter. That is what he needed. So we sat beneath the tree. We rooted ourselves. I didn't need to tell him that under the roots was nothing. They grew so long that they touched space and stars. This time he laughed because he saw that upon my heart and he knew that we both knew. That was spirit's gift to us. We have always wound our way to a path where eventually we could see the same truths and not even use words to explain it. In every way, we listened to each other's heart. That is our forever language. When I was a dog, it was the same and I acted even before he spoke. His friends said, "She can read your mind, she must be part human!" I still smile because I always would reply that he was part dog. But that is another dream.

We sat with that tree and we melded. We shaped ourselves into clouds. We blew ourselves into winds. We arched ourselves into mountains. We blued ourselves into skies. We became every part of ourselves. We chameleoned our bodies. That was my way of saying to him, "Thomas, I come again and again. It is so easy to find a body and to shape it. We already have the same heart. That's the hard part. It is much simpler to come into new forms and to find ourselves together again. There is no way we could miss each other."

    I do not ask how he heard me. I only know that he did. His spirit stands very strong and when it is his time it tells him everything. He holds nothing away because he has committed to touch love through everything.

    Even while the Hannah body molded into the earth, I traveled the blue sky road to Thomas. His eyes looked sad. It was as if my coming now was a reminder of something he couldn't quite touch. Deep within him, he never forgot. And our place of love stayed safe, but still, he was human. His hand was still reaching across space and time to hold my heart. And I wanted to give it to him just exactly as he asked. One more time.

Two

Time passes in the human world. I don't know why. But then, I have never worried enough to find out. I decided to wrap my beautiful essence into an new equally beautiful body.

Have you guessed?

Yes, it was a dog body. A black and white malamute puppy with the same stance as Hannah. By now, Thomas was full of love. Most of the grief had passed and his heart stretched wide to know even more beauty. He found the openness to give more of himself again. He found a woman to live with him. So I went to the woman. I went to her by a dream and I said, "Come and get me. I can be a piece of your love. I can make you a family."

She did. She found me just as she was instructed, and even thought it was her own idea. I suppose that it was. And she took me right to Thomas. The family began again.

    I wish you could have seen him. His eyes grew wide. For one moment, he shone like the sun. I knew it was my time again. I ran and I played like Hannah. I listened like her. Because I was her. For one more time.

    Yet, the body was new. Like all sacred things it had started all over again. My spirit. My love. My life. So I asked for a new name and they gave it to me. I was called Tundra Spruce. From that moment on, I left Hannah in the ghost of a dream. And I wore Tundra Spruce into a new world.

    That is how you find me now. Almost. I have come here to give you my story because the gift of Thomas in my spirit allows me to speak the ancient ways and the words of the future as well. We of animal and of human skins, we are coming together. And I have been given this place of honor to speak of how I have come to share all my love with Thomas.

    In my speaking, perhaps you will find yourself. You may find yourself in love with all beings again. That is our spirits talking ... But that is for another sunrise when I will come to you again ...

Three

Hello. I am Tundra. Thank you for being here. I have agreed to tell my story at long last. But before I go into it I have to tell you that the telling isn't for me. I didn't come here so you could know who I am. I don't care about that. My story is here because I gave it away. Right from the beginning of it, I gave away my heart. It sounds odd to you humans. For me, it means I have assured myself of love. I know I will live and die every single day, knowing all the love that is possible for me to be. So I gave away these words a long time ago. I agreed that I would not speak until I could give my whole life story to Thomas and now he has given it to you. I pray that it will be good medicine on your earth-walk.

Now, back to my life. I was a loyal and serious puppy. I followed Thomas everywhere. Every chance I got, I stepped right on his feet because I wanted to feel his footprints. I wanted to feel the heartbeat in his feet as it touched the earth.

"Can't you walk somewhere else," he hollered at me. I smiled, even as I bowed before him trembling. His heart reached out and touched mine. No matter what he said, that was the language between us. So I always followed that first. And to this day, I slip into his footprints. To this day, he still hollers at me.

How can I tell you, any of you, that I don't mind. For me it is beyond caring. I pledge my heart to him. I know this first, and last, and through and through. Stepping on him seems to be a part of it sometimes. Thomas is a free being and I don't own him. His liking or not liking my actions in any moment is also part of that pledge. I worship it all, though you may not think so. I am a free being too. I have always been so and I believe that I choose this forever. I have chosen to love all parts of him and I am fortunate that he lets me see and touch all of him. Even the ones that sometimes seem hard. While I tell you this, I am also telling him.

I came to know all of this love. I specifically came to know every part of his heart as my own. When it comes to hearts, they beat the same rhythm over and over. They have given me their wisdom. Do you know why they can hold that pulse day after day, year after year? It's because they have so completely entered their own being, they have turned themselves inside out. They know who they are and they bless it without a single thought. Each heart comes into a body to express love. It is everything.

The day that Thomas touched Hannah's heart, it jumped back to life. It resurrected. That body, even though it was tired, even though it was time for it to go, it came back because it knew such love that nothing in its being could say no. For a few seconds, and probably a real lifetime, it flooded. My being slipped into Thomas' hands. Then I was absolutely alive. I became my purpose. In that moment, I freely presented to him every breath, every quality, of my core self.

He accepted. I saw his spirit over his shoulder. It was the last sight in Hannah's eyes. When Thomas asked for one more time, his spirit nodded and said, "Will you join me for timelessness?"

I said, "Yes!"

Four

Timelessness is everything.

It's all my stories, right here, right now.

To talk with you, I choose one part of me to be. That doesn't mean that I forget the others. I see my other bodies. They lay with me. Some chase around my tail. Little whispers come in my ears with our secrets. Those are the other me's. I visit them all and they me, and we are our whole family.

As Tundra, I gave that family to Thomas. He's looking at me right now. He sees a black wolf, a very skittish coyote, and well, many …… I would rather let them tell you who they are themselves.

I am happy for my human family to look upon me and to recognize me. With all my heart, I invite all of you other humans to really see me and to hear me. As a show of my trust, I give you my power name. It is Ogallalah de Oro. The wind carries it now and that is enough for me.

18   Ogallalah de Oro

Just call me Ogallalah.

This is my name now. Ogallalah holds the timelessness. Sends it through the dog-body. I hope you can see it. It hugs the earth and cries into the sky. I have prepared myself long to be called this. Every time my name is spoken, timelessness touches us. My story then comes out in one way or another. Just like this.

As Ogallalah, I can tell you about every time I have walked upon the earth. To me, all of my selves are walking upon the earth. It is so beautiful and full here. It fills my nose and I am always home.

Meet me as the black wolf. That was when I lived in the northwest part of this continent. I roamed so many places because I was very big. I had no desire to be a part of a pack. I ate and slept with myself. How can I explain to you? I was a spirit animal for a tribe of people for all of that life. I looked for them. I smelled them in the earth, but I never met them. One night I howled into the moon. I so wanted to lay with them in the night. To feel their skin touch me in wonder. I felt I already knew each of them by name and by scent. I could have hunted them in my sleep but they were just beyond me. Always a little ways ahead.

"Why do you howl for them?" the moon asked.

"Because they are in my blood. I know they are my family."

She laughed. She laughed at me. I was so serious I listened for them even closer. Hhmmmm.

"Lonely wolf," She laughed again, "Don't you see? The smell in your nose is their touch. Their faces and feelings inside of you are indelible. You already walk with them. You have been designated as the outer circle guardian."

I bowed. It is so sacred to have the moon speak your life to you. I buried my nose in the earth so that her words would mingle in that coolness and never leave.

She went on, "You don't need to stand next to them to stand *with* them. You are so lucky. You are showing them the way to travel in the earth. They are following you even when they can't track you. Your spirit looms large before them. They see you, talk to you, and can never be lost because of you. Wherever you go, there is food, there is water, and there is love. What more could you want?"

The answer to that came to me just like everything else, in its own way and in its own season. I no longer wait for anything.

Five

As Tundra, I grew into myself. Hannah went on to be a different guardian so that Tundra Spruce could be a different kind of tree. I was delighted to know Thomas. Each day we would see the sun together. I got a bone first thing in the morning and that's as good as anything I could imagine. And I would feel him wherever he was. Usually, I got to travel with him. He would drive, but I would help. My essence sings as a guardian. It finds a flow into every other living thing when I am protecting. To look after something, for me, is like the rain falling, the flowers blooming. It is everything in its place.

Sometimes it was too much for Thomas. My nose in his face was too strong. Not many humans can smell and send their words in the smell. The ones who are alive in their dogness or wolfness, they do this without thinking. That's Thomas. I overpowered him with that much vitality and sharpness of senses. Can you other humans see it? Sometimes he snapped with impatience. Sometimes he hugged me and said, "I can't imagine anything without you!"

What a combination! I was delirious. To feel all those things at once is a sensory explosion for me. In every feeling, I could sense part of him listening to his emotions. Touching them. Playing them. Talking them. Liking them. Not liking them. Sending them away. These were my many gifts in our partnership.

I was about two years as Tundra when the visits began. I am kin to the grandmother with the long braids, the white robe, and the human skin. In the full moon, she would lay next to me. She whispered in my ear, "You have never been lonely. Your family is growing and growing."

I suppose you're wondering what that means. I never did. Every time the woman came to me, my body grew firmer and happier. Change was being born in me and I knew that my season was coming. As a guardian, I became more insistent. Had to be wherever Thomas was. An ancient longing stalked me. Wolf smell hung in the air. My instincts asked me to stand between Thomas and anyone else nearby. I didn't hurt anyone. I had no desire to do so. I just knew that my body needed to share his space. It had something to give him. When we were next to each other I knew that our spirits talked and loved. I did anything to allow this and then, it happened.

His woman love left our house. The sadness was so complete I could see a sun setting in his eyes. I understood. The whisperings of my night visitor made me ready. I laid alongside of Thomas each night. When he was asleep I let my heart talk in the ways I have been taught, but almost couldn't imagine. "Thomas, you have given away the part of your heart that was not free. You have cut away the piece that was tied and dying. Don't you see, you were being a reflection of someone's need because you knew how to, not because it was your place? You have made a warm space in your heart. It is a new home. I am the outer circle guardian who has come in. I will help you to find more family. I cannot give them to you. You are too free for that. But I will point them out. I will speak to them first. I will go ahead and leave you visions in the night so that you will recognize where you will finally be home."

Six

It takes so much from me to give you these words. I have to reach deep into the earth. I need to feel that coolness on my face. I need to smell like her heart, so that I can feel the rhythm of how to tell my story. Everything I say is a part of the earth's spinning, the sun's travels. I pull it out from my own belly so you can know all of that. If sometimes it doesn't make sense to you, or if sometimes I am not humanly eloquent, it is because I tear my being from everything I have known. It overwhelms words. It is guts and smells. Everything here is everything I have done, going right into everything I will ever do. If you can't quite keep pace with me, it's o.k. You have another place in the earth's seasons and I'm sure you are finding it.

Thomas was in the season of grief. To feel it was making him more alive. I could see old hurts lifting out of his bodies. Sometimes they had faces. I knew that they were his old family telling him who he wasn't. I licked him constantly. Especially when he didn't let me. Those old ghosts needed to be cleaned. It wasn't their fault that they were old stories. They were leaving. I said goodbye and made space for the new ones.

    I sent him three dreams of the braided woman. One night he woke up. I didn't move. I could feel him reaching out to touch her just as I had done when I was hunting for my tribe. His eyes widened and widened. He looked for her beyond the shadows. I think he cried for a very long time. The moon talked him back to sleep and I knew we had found each other in a new way.

Seven

The next day, when I looked at him, the spirits around him smiled and pointed at me. They laughed, so I barked. He said, "You know what we're doing, don't you? It's time. We are going to have puppies. Is it all right? Will you be o.k.?"

Thomas sat cross-legged next to me. There were stones all around us. My body alerted every sense. I was Mother. I had been declared so by a circle of beings that we had yet to talk to. I was going to have my own family.

On April 15, I gave birth to seven babies. Thomas paced. He carried them from my birth canal and gave them to me to lick. What a fine adventure for humans and dogs! For every one, he smiled and said, "Hello, look at you, you are so beautiful!"

It was work to push out the big babies. My body got just tired enough that my primal senses came to the front. I saw each pup take their first breath. And the Mother spirit in me saw everything else. Their lives unfolded in front of me. I could see where they were going. I could see the colors of what they were like, around them.

Though I knew Thomas could sense it, I didn't try to tell him that one of the babies wouldn't live long. It was an offering to the earth. He was meant to breathe just enough to take that back with him. Thomas was quiet when he found the dead puppy the next morning. I looked at him. He looked at me. We knew that we had felt it coming in our bellies. It pained him and I knew that he would let it go just as quickly as it could.

I fed and I watched the others. I followed them everywhere. We played outside in the yard. I told each one to stay away from the road. They listened, but they were new to their bodies and I knew they were listening to the stars and to everything else. So I got louder. I whined and I snorted and I ran over them. After all, I am a guardian. Whatever life was entrusted to me, I took care of it, Thomas included.

It may sound strange to you, but he was inside every puppy. They wriggled and they played for the part of him (Thomas) that needed to be little and still safe. He even looked like them. I don't remember anybody else noticing the resemblance, but the eyes of every being are different. You know what I mean. I know that you do. Those puppies were spinning colors and while they lived with us, Thomas and I spun in our own colors. We were a family that knew no time.

Eight

Oh'hne. It means infinity. She named herself in an ancient circle of fire and whispered it to Thomas three weeks after she was born.

Luckily he heard her and he knew that she was the puppy that was going to stay and live with us.

In our bodies, Oh'hne and I did not need to be close. I was the guardian. That was my sacred place in the family. If you saw me just once you would know this. Oh'hne, she was the freedom that was coming in like a lightning bolt. She danced around the house. Sparks sailed through the air. Her sacred place was to make more room for all the others coming. I knew that she was not as interested in being touched. For that matter, she was not overly attached to her dog-body. She knew it was a vessel from which many other kinds of beings would speak. You would have known it to look at her. She was black and white, long furred, with a pink star at the end of her nose.

As she grew, she did not especially look like me. But that was because she didn't need me. I had my job, ***and clearly***, she had hers. Nothing would stop either of us!

I kept her in line every minute and she pushed the line just around the edges. Oh'hne didn't mind the rules because she heard voices from other tribes. They advised her. She had her own family that was coming to join her and then to join us.

Nine

    Thomas is full of everything. He lives with every feeling he has ever had. And even when he doesn't want to, he lives with everyone else's feelings, too. That's why he knows what I want and what I need. I fit this rhythm in him. I don't know if he knows this, but Oh'hne emptied him out.

    No matter how much he hurt, she would tease open his heart. She would paw at his spirit endlessly. She pulled him out from himself and showed him another world. I watched them at night when they were dreaming. Oh'hne walked into her horse body. No matter what he was dreaming, she would dance right in on it. She sang to him in a high, light voice and he would follow her. They traveled the whole night – Thomas and the horse that was named Infinity. I stayed by the bed and made sure they were all safe.

    One day, fall was in the air. Our sumac burst into scarlet. Everything was set just so. I smiled at Oh'hne.

Ogallalah de Oro

She knew. It wasn't a secret to us. We knew she was coming. Oh'hne and I raced around the yard. This was going to be a very special harvest season. The woman who was coming now was blood and spirit and clan to us. Everything in our bodies was ready. Oh'hne made a nest in the yard and rolled in it. We were excited but not anticipating. The seasons of love were unfolding around us just as they needed to be.

She came to our house. Thomas introduced us. We already knew that she was Marilyn. I watched her stand next to Oh'hne. They were exactly the same. There wasn't any need to note the resemblance, but from that moment on, wherever Marilyn walked, Oh'hne did, too. And long after she left the house, she was still in Oh'hne's eyes and stayed with us ever after.

Thomas and Marilyn were timeless. I could see that. Everything could see that. Of course, they had to find that out a piece at a time so that the old hurts could slip away easily and make more room for each other. Hhhmmmm.... by the way, I was never jealous; I'm not sure many dogs really are. You may think that about us, but we only act upon whatever roles you present to us. I knew that my role would never be the same. I liked it. Before she left the house that day, I walked out with her. She went to her car and I stopped at the front door. She turned around, startled that I did not follow her all the way to her car. Our eyes looked into each others' hearts and I gave her everything that was there, "Please do not come back to him until you know what you are doing!"

Ten

I know that saying those words really brought her up short. I could feel her lurch in her body and find the bond between her and Thomas strong and undeniable. Yet, if I hadn't said that, and if she hadn't listened, well, maybe she would have denied it for some time. That would have been painful for Thomas because his feelings had already risen out of his body and were freely flowing in the air between them.

No matter what, I am a guardian. And I did what was my sacred duty to do. There was no malice or judgment for me. Just the honoring of all the truths between us spoken or otherwise.

Let me explain. For many humans, guardian means someone who will fight. It conjures up pictures of a very aggressive being ready to die for them. While I would die if I had to, I choose to live through everything so that I can keep helping. I am the final support. That's my job. As a guardian I don't fight off what is painful or demanding. With my dog alertness I simply point out everything that seems to be creating conflict. I touch the hidden feelings. I allow them to come to the surface with all my love. When they are in the open they can be dealt with, they can be nurtured, or they can be sent to new homes. Fighting them is what makes the war inside go on. I honor Thomas beyond that (That's probably my whole story right there!).

As for Marilyn, she joined our family not too long after that. She came into our house on a day when fires raged in the nearby countryside. I will always smell her as something burning. To me, she is hot and immediate and a vision of what is coming. Oh'hne and I formed a circle around the house and when she finally came it was late at night. We knew that she came with the moon's instincts. There were dreams all around her. I could have touched them but they were not mine. They were Oh'hne's.

I am guardian for all of my family but it is the desire in Thomas' body that asks me to stand over him most of all. I do. Can you understand, it is not a contest. No conflict resides in my body. I love them all and I love my duty as well.

Oh'hne stands over Marilyn. Their bodies link whenever they share the same space. You would think it funny because they hardly seem to notice each other. They do not play often. But it was that sure independence that was their root. In their deepest bellies, they beat with it and they smiled, because they matched their rhythms, day by day, and night by night. When I look upon Marilyn I see the same pink star on her face. I know, just as I breathe, that they both are very ancient family. I see them birthing each other. I see Oh'hne mothering her and Marilyn mothering Oh'hne. They are a long line of females who have done it so often and so well that they no longer need to do it. So they are detached in a primal attachment. They can come and go with their nurturing. I am learning this from them (They are learning from me, in their almost careless, and, yes, carefree, running over of lines and sacred space, not to run over our hearts. Perhaps that is Thomas' duty as well.).

As you may have sensed, there are many periods of time in my story. Some come to you like past pieces. Some are now and some are glorious hints of what is coming. To me they are all now as well. I tell you this because as I speak these holy words, these bits of life lay in my past. They have already happened, but because my spirit draws them out of the depths of my soul, now, they are right now! I am living it again, totally, completely. I am living it freely because I do not wallow in any of the feelings. I let it all rush over me like an ocean wave. It completely envelops me. I absorb it into my being and then it is gone. No traces.

I wanted you to know this because as you live my story with me I want to give you that. Here, take this feeling of being drowned in every feeling. You can know what it is to let it wash you clean and in the next moment all that is left is your clear being. When you live so completely, the sun passes right through you and everything else does too. It means that every primal emotion which exists in all of us, travels through you and doesn't make war. Consider that. Then everything, no matter what time it seems to spring from, is brand new and leaves no traces. I hope you like my gift!

Many things happened after Thomas and Marilyn joined. We left the home in the city and we ran to the woods in the north. Oh'hne appeared like a red-haired maiden in Thomas' dream. She was secretly half horse. She came to him by full moon and smiled the night away with him, and just before sunrise she whispered, "The land by the lake is ready now. Go to her." Even in his sleep he tried to stand up. At that, Oh'hne disappeared. That day, we all decided to move.

Oh'hne and I ran through the woods. She hunted and I chased after assorted wild beings. After all, I was still the guardian. Oh'hne was my daughter and I felt that I had to be there to watch after her. Most of all, I watched Marilyn and Thomas. Not so much watched after, I noticed them. I saw them unfold into a new being every day. Thomas walked the land steadily. His eyes grew sharper. Whenever that happens I know that it is his curiosity carving its way into a new unknown. He was forging a path and all the creatures and the spirits of the trees were with him. All of a sudden, he had more guardians than maybe he could have imagined.

I saw them all.

Since I didn't have to worry about imagination, these beings just walked up to me. We knew each other and we lived together. There were stars and sprites. There was a mist from the lake with thousands of names. One day they discovered her and called her Rocktafhar. For them, it was an amazing beginning. They were falling and flying into a world that I had welcomed them to a long time ago.

Every dawn, Rocktafhar would ease through the trees. She guided our family of spirits. She looked over us all. Thomas decided I was more relaxed than he had ever imagined. I was simply being my place in the tribe. Each moment it formed fresh. It passed through me and left no traces.

Every night, the four of us walked through the woods. Oh'hne ran ahead. She could never resist a new smell. I told her that it was important for us to stay a little bit close. She laughed at me. Oh'hne was forever laughing at me. Even when I would collar her and put her body into belly submission, her giggles would run through the air like little bells. It was a dance between us. I was the drawing of the circle where inside of it, everything was safe. She was the jump over it into the stars. Isn't it a beautiful rhythm?

    As we strolled by bushes, trees and strawberries, and later, high snowbanks, I felt the primal (I don't know what to call it in your language, so I will say, reflexes.), reflexes, I felt them percolating in Marilyn's body restlessly. Ancient – forever voices stirred in her womb. I knew there had to be a birth coming very soon.

My Favorite Flowers
calla lilly
casa blanca lilly

Monday
11

Wolves have three eyelids. Along with the regular top and bottom lid found in humans, a wolf has a clear layer that protects the eye from dust.

July

S	M	T	W	T	F	S
					1	2
3	4	5	6	7	8	9
10	11	12	13	14	15	16
17	18	19	20	21	22	23
24	25	26	27	28	29	30
31						

©AGC, Inc.

Eleven

One day, our whole life changed. It only takes one day. One second of infinity. Whatever came before this disappeared. What was, dropped out from underneath us, and we floated into space.

Come with me now and feel it.

It was spring in the woods. Lots of green. Lots of earth moistness filled our senses. The air transformed itself. It was no longer light or invisible. I watched as it carried currents all around our little house. Golden bolts circled. They danced the trees. They certainly alerted all of the animals. They pushed the birds into songs, new songs. Premonition had come to us. It awakened something in Thomas and Marilyn that had never been asleep. When they noticed, the birth began.

At dusk that day, they pledged their bodies to all of their spirit families. They gave their voice to them and sat back in awe. They trembled from deep inside them. I stayed very close. So did Oh'hne. We had witnessed many initiations like this. This was like an animal's rite of passage to claim their place in the pack or in the family. I say that it was like the animals' because we animals stay tuned to those communications that aren't just human only. We keep our instincts sharp regardless of all the breeding and domestication. That's how we live in your world, in our world, and in the place where the spirits talk to all of us the same.

Oh'hne and I were wilder than many dogs. That was by design. We were bringing the language of our elders and our clan to humans. So we needed to be awake. We had to live on the edge of our instincts so that we could give that to Thomas and to Marilyn and finally to you.

That's what happened that night. The gift of all the other languages, or maybe it is the one core language, passed through us into their bodies. I witnessed this. I recorded this so that it could be translated into humanspeak. While they sat in the cabin and felt their etheric guides, inside as well as outside of them, I stood guard. This was my place in the family.

Two blue whirlwinds descended upon them. There was electricity snapping back and forth. They entered the tops of their heads and spun every thought that they believed in. Thomas' hands glowed red. I could feel the heat. White beliefs leaked out of Marilyn's feet. Old whispers that said, "I am not enough, I am not this, I cannot do this," were asked to leave. No voices came out of either of them and they seemed a bit disappointed but everything was set in place. The language of all of us was already coursing through them.

Twelve

A new adventure had begun. As soon as Marilyn and Thomas had given their voices to spirits around them, those beings grew very large in their lives. Even before they could speak with them, Oh'hne and I greeted the new family.

We saw every kind of being walking with us. There were trolls and gnomes and rocks, and bigger than anything, were the trees growing into each other and waving. I spoke with each of them. Sometimes I even rolled around their etheric bodies to put their scent in my fur. I wanted to help make them familiar to my human family.

This world has never been strange to me. Trees have always talked to me. It is part of breathing, but I know that for many humans, it seems odd. They think that if the words aren't out loud in their language, then there is no communication. Even further, they feel there is no consciousness then.

     All of my life as Ogallalah, I have steadily recorded the non-word language of the land and the creatures. It pours/pores through my skin. It warms my body. It flows through my heart until it isn't just my heart anymore. Every time I walk or I eat or I sleep, a thousand stories have come into me. I feel them all. I love them for coming to me and making me a part of them and for birthing me.

     Now, I give them back to everything else that can hear. I send the rock-stories out to every one of you. I know their consciousness and they have given you their stories so you can find your consciousness inside of them. That is part of their life destiny. It is part of mine. That is why I am here now. It is part of *Twintreess*, as well.

     Soon, their (Thomas' and Marilyn's) bodies adjusted to all spirit whisperings. The stories came out through their own voices. Some of them spilled onto paper, just like this one. They opened up their hearts and Pleiadeans spoke through them. Actually, everything came to share their love in new words. It was a gift for all of us.

Thirteen

Oh'hne stepped right in. Nothing ever held her back. As a matter of fact, she didn't wait for the new speaking process. She went to Thomas and Marilyn and spoke anyway.

"I'm not going to live long. I'm getting ready for the next world."

Thomas said, "But you only have another six months until you are three, then you would be old enough to have puppies."

She was delighted! "I will wait for that! It would be an adventure to have babies."

Thomas pledged, "Then that's what we will do."

When Oh'hne came into her heat, they listened to her heart. She told them who she wished to mate. When. And, she told them, "I will have four or five puppies. They will be big, so I am still arranging it. I will let you know later."

So Thomas and Marilyn planned it. They made dates for us to visit the father but the woman who owned the stud cancelled several times. Finally, on a full moon day, we all went and Oh'hne was bred.

Again, she didn't wait. She mated instantly and came back to the truck where we were all huddled together. Normally, Marilyn and Thomas sit in the front and we dogs have the back to ourselves. This day, Marilyn sat next to me. Oh'hne curled tightly into a ball to hold the new life inside her. Marilyn looked into her eyes. I saw her (Marilyn) start because she could see what we could see. The eyes of the puppies were already behind Oh'hne's stare. All of our bodies were changed. We were all going to give birth.

Fourteen

I called in all of the spirits to dance around us. I sang to my mother, who sang to her mother. They protected us. Their wings encircled the land where we made ready to make more family upon the earth.

I would like for you to feel this from my bones to yours. I am Ogallalah, guardian. Oh'hne was growing her children and I was growing my love around all of us. It is why I was alive. It is why I still live. I shall not leave this body as long as there is need for the protection that is so much a part of my breath, my heart, and my soul.

As I give you these sacred words, they are winging around you. Our circle grows and yet heightens to bring us together. You are my family, my new family as well. I am the mother-spirit walking through a dog-form. I give you all that I am so that none of us will be less.

Oh'hne rounded. She played less and watched the sky for the help that was already there. I, too, watched the sky, to see the owls who would come when new little ones would stagger about our home. The warmth in my soul rose each day. I was like the sun to Oh'hne and she was like the moon to us all, and the children would be the flowers of the earth. I know, just as I know how to breathe, or how to howl, that each of these puppies was special. Those bodies would never be copied and only a certain spirit would walk in them. Only the spirits who called out to those forms with open hearts would enter them. I watched as they grew further and further into their forms, while I grew into Grandmother.

    I do not age because I do not count. I leap into the next cycle. I do not know the cycle until it knows me. This way it is all newness for me to wear grandmother and it is also all ancientness. Every time finds itself. So it flows through me and gives me blood to pump.

    June Nineteenth, the only day that could hold all five of these beings, the forest echoed lightwinds. Sun reflected off the land and the bed lay ready for the time of pain and wonder.

    I circled around the house as I had been taught to do by a teacher I no longer remembered. Drums and whistles sang in tree leaves. I carried their gifts proudly into the house, gifts for the grandchildren.

    Marilyn was pacing, back and forth, back and forth. It was as if she could understand the vibrations in her womb speaking to Oh'hne's, "We are all women-mothers. We rock with you as the earth rocks, now."

    I met her eyes. She did not know that she moved for Oh'hne. Her human thoughts could not tell her, but blood is primal and it was already in the air. I sat by her and guarded her, even though she did not ask, while she wrote words of labor and aching that wrote themselves. When the last word left her heart, the first child dropped from Oh'hne's body. Oh'hne appreciated the writing-ritual-welcome.

Though I have never spoken of this to any human, it was that poem that pulled the firstborn into outer life. He was a boy. He heard his song. It called out to him and gave him the impetus to breathe outside of his mother and to know his own body.

Welcome.

Oh'hne was and is fast. She is captured fire with lightning moving through her. Three more babies fell from her womb onto the human and dog and spirit-made bed. Then the fight for life began. I prayed. I did not pray for life or for death or for any particular event. I formed the holy words because they were inside of me and asked to be sung out. Never have I questioned the breath of spirit.

Its scream swung through the air. Oh'hne paced. Tight circles and sparks formed her shield. The last puppy was the biggest of all. He was strong. He was and is a warrior incarnate, but too gentle to rip his mother to be free. I have never asked Thomas and Marilyn if they understood what he said to us. I know they hear all, just as you do and just as you do now.

"Grandmother and Mother, I stretch the circle of life around me so your body can grow and give me passage to the air. I do not ask you to hurt for me. I ask for all that I am to come through. There is no more."

Thomas turned to Marilyn, "Is there someone we can talk to? Is there someone there who can help?"

They huddled and listened. Takroo came. His kindness translated, "We will all birth this last one. All of these children have been a union of all the kingdoms upon the earth. Human, plant, animal, spirit, all. The last one cannot leave the mother until we recognize the sacredness and chant the end of the litter."

Thomas drummed. Now we all paced. But it was

filled in meaning and intent. We gave the rhythm to Oh'hne's heart and moved the last child who had not yet turned. We were ready. He was ready, and he sprung forth into our world. We knew we were all alive.

Fifteen

By the next day, I planted myself into the new bed of the new family. I laid over and tried to give them milk. Thomas shooed me out, "These are not your babies. Oh'hne needs to feed them now. You can go and find your own place."

I laid outside the door. I had already found my place. Oh'hne was not going to stay long with the babies and I was ready to show them that I could care for them at any time. My body was dry of milk and full of need to give them wholeness. So, I gave to them at each moment. They were a sacred circle and nothing in their nurturance was broken.

Thomas and Marilyn spoke to the little ones in their own way. They heard each one pick a home to live in and humans to teach. Their message was eternal. They brought the union of all beings into each life they touched.

Oh'hne's body felt tired. All of her fur dropped,

well, most of it, and it returned slowly. Her voice did not waver, "I have done what I asked to do. I already see the next adventure. It's touching me. It's loving me and I cannot resist it."

Thomas said, "Would you like to stay to have another litter?"

"You mean in my next cycle?"

"No. Your body isn't recovered yet. You can still regenerate and be ready in the next one after that."

She smiled, "I will not be here to live through another heat."

Sixteen

I invigorate in the fall. I enliven in it. My fur tingles and I am what I was designed for – a creature to travel in cold without struggle.

To Thomas and Marilyn, it was the first Sunday of deer hunting season. The woods around us trembled. I smelled blood, but it was not deer. The humans told us to stay near. They worried about the guns and the dogs that looked like wolves. I had no need for these words as I had no need to run.

Oh'hne came to me. She was part dream, part sunlight. With respect, she said, "Goodbye! I go my way alone and there I will meet everyone."

She ran into the trees. Though she was not the same color as the woods, she turned brown and red and orange. Her power made her invisible and I set her free.

That does not mean that I was responsible for her journey. It means that her body left mine just as it needed to be. So it was.

That night, Oh'hne did not come to the door to come inside the house. She had never done this.

In the spirit world, the pacing had already begun. Thomas was worried. He called for her. Marilyn laid in the bed and argued within herself that she did not feel differently.

They hunted for her the next few days but she could not be found. So they touched her in the spirit speaking. She gave them her story. "I'm in the woods. You cannot come to me. You cannot help me. I am an initiate. I have chosen this way. I ask you not to interfere."

Marilyn and Thomas heard words that said Oh'hne had found a hunter's trap, poisoned bait. She had eaten it, swallowed it, and then she could not release it. She lay in the woods away from them, dying as herself.

Thomas cried. I stayed close. He cried more and implored her, "If you are going to die now, we respect that. Can you do it here with us? We want to hold your body one last time. We want to feel you in our fingers so that your impression will meld with our instincts and our reflexes. Then we will know you whenever we are moved to do so."

Silence.

Seventeen

I watched. I danced in waiting. I saw Thomas' heart lead. I welcomed in the sun. I welcomed in the moon. Because it felt like my place to be. He counted the days instead.

Day five in eternity without Oh'hne.

It was only natural to me, because everything is. With all his breath gathered, Thomas sat next to me, "Please, she's your daughter. Can you take us to her? We will not stop her. We cannot. We accept her choice. We want to be a part of it."

Marilyn was fasting. She had not eaten for a couple of days. Her body still matched Oh'hne's. As long as there was breath between them, they moved in the same darkness, in the same light. They traveled like sisters.

That night, all of us tuned in to Oh'hne. The moon came out full, just as it had in the last birthing in this family. She crept inside of Marilyn's body. I witnessed for all beings wherever they were.

Huge shivers passed through her uncontrolled. Oh'hne's voice lurched out loud and then almost inaudibly. I heard it all! I hear it forever!

"I go now. I must! All adventures begin by ending the last one. I declare, I am Oh'hne. I am the endless circle. It is my destiny to be the end weaving into the beginning into the end, always. It is my life, just as this is my death."

Gasps escaped from Marilyn. The last breaths had begun.

"It is alright. Even though it sounds hard, I want to talk to you. I want to share this mystery with you. Even though my body can barely pulse, I give this to you. I want to give this, all of this. It is part of why I came and it will send me on an adventure where you will know more and more of me."

Thomas cried aloud, "Can we find your body? Can you show us the way to it? I would like to put it into the earth so I will still know that you are safe and that you are ever loved in any form."

She smiled. "You cannot find where I am now."

Eighteen

They counted two days in grief. Tears washed away the traces of Oh'hne that had already moved on. And then there were even more tears. They remembered aloud the last time they enjoyed the sight of Oh'hne. She had danced in the night, in the light of their headlights, as they came home to be a family for the last time. Oh'hne had bucked and whirled, leaped like a horse.

I had watched the stallion in her always. It continually surprised Thomas and Marilyn. Their laughter was sweet. For a little while, Oh'hne would lay dead in their hearts. It was their ritual. It was their humanness planted in the earth and reaching for the stars. Part of them pretended not to understand, while the rest of them knew and knew.

Then we all traveled. Thomas had a sound chamber to build. He drove us all to Wisconsin. We were quiet. They rested the spirit speaking and went inside to find themselves. I could smell newness in the air. We went to a place where Oh'hne's firstborn son lived. This was not planned in the human sense or even in the dog sense. It was designed from the depths of all beings, so we could meet ourselves, so we could remember family in the ancient ways, and then give it away peacefully.

They spoke with Bear, her son. I saw his shadow larger than the trees. They saw a shaman. He could not speak until spoken to, as was arranged from forever. Thomas looked at his ritual garb, "Welcome Bear Shaman."

He nodded.

"Can you speak to us of Oh'hne?"

The feathers from Bear's headdress flew into a smoky breeze and when it left, the feathers lay like ashes upon the earth. Each feather planted itself and another shaman returned from the invisible places. They danced slow and heavy around us carrying the sadness. They, too, smiled. Bear waited and then spoke. "I cannot waste words. All my intent and all my energy goes with my mother. I honor her journey by not speaking until one week has passed."

Nineteen

One week passed. The humans assembled after supper. I could feel the anxiety inside their bodies. It was like a visitor speaking to me but it was invisible to them. I brought myself to full attention. They formed a circle. Marilyn emptied herself to feel the light touch of Oh'hne's feather spirit. As was decreed, Bear, who laid outside in the snow, stood with all his being to project, and he howled like a dog in a shaman. He howled and the humans heard his words again, "I will not speak until one week has passed."

We of instinctual bodies do not measure our lives. We live ourselves and the seasons tell us when to act. It is all there is. Bear could not live outside his honor.

Oh'hne traveled back to lay kindness on Marilyn's and Thomas' ears. "Hello." There were no trembles, no gasps. "It is me, Oh'hne, and I love you all."

The tears on Marilyn's face were her own.

Thomas's tears were to hold love in all the pain.

"I left my body and I went down a path. I knew that it was just for me. I knew that I could only go because you had finally set me free. I was already free! So I leaped down the path! And then everything inside of me quieted. My breaths were echoes. Every moment passed through me like a season of infinity. I could not trace it, nor did I want to. So I walked in sacredness. On either side of me, I saw fires spring up! Around the fires were beings. Some were human. Some were animal. Some were unimaginable. All of them were family. Everywhere I looked, there was somebody I knew that I had forgotten and that I had remembered. You can't imagine how much family we have! They were there for me. Such a feeling! I cannot give it words, because I cannot hold it long enough. Our family did not come to me. They stayed around the fires. They shone at me, Oh'hne. I knew they were holding me in respect. It was my time of initiation. No hands could hold me up. Only trust could carry me. It was almost lonely. Almost. I needed to rest, even though I'm not sure that I was tired. I laid down and looked up. The moon loomed larger and larger. It filled the sky and squeezed out the blue. It shimmered down to me. I was being held. She laid with me but took nothing from me. We were both free beings. We understood each other and we smiled at the void of white. Then it was gone. I was walking again. My mute family moved their eyes with my every step. They knew what was coming because it was not their time! It was my moment and they could see it coming to mate with me. I closed my eyes. My ears pricked in the wind, but there was no moving air. I saw then, I saw, I saw, ohh, I saw it! Even though you will hear this, as though I did one thing and then the next, this is not how it was for me. I was and I became the movement of my journey complete. I saw, and in the same moment, I ran. I ran and I saw. The path dropped into nothingness. Every cell in me pushed me through. I ached, but I could not remember pain. I leapt into it! I leapt into nothing!"

She paused here as everything enveloped her again.

"The only way I can explain it to you, is that I became my initiation. I leapt into it. Even though it was not a familiar fire, I propelled myself into it. When everything I knew fell away, I flew! Guess what? I was a red horse! I love red! Because my eyes were wide open, I landed in seven worlds simultaneously! They caught me and I landed them. I had seven new bodies to live. And because I had met my fate as myself freely, I remembered Oh'hne. I spoke Oh'hne in all seven languages. Not everyone heard it, but I did! I gave up forgetting. I was all of them and I would never leave that behind. How can I thank you? Don't you see? I heard you when you said, 'We accept all your choices unconditionally. We will not ask you to stay for us.' That was the magic! That was the magic that birthed myself to me. I am my own puppy and my own mother and other things that I invite you to feel whenever you are ready to. That's another story! I love you so much. I don't love you because you let me go. I love you because I am me. The more me I am, the more love I give to you. Can I tell you? It's free! It is so wonderful here! I can hardly bring thoughts to lines to leave with you. Dad, can you see me? I'm a butterfly! I'm all white and gold and I'm anything that you imagine me to be! I can dance with or without the light. The light's inside me! That's what my body was trying to tell you that night in your headlights. The light passed through me. It's inside and outside. Dying again has given me life. I hope you can know this! I hope you can feel it. I won't ask you not to cry. It doesn't touch me. I am so happy! I am so everything at once! If only Oh'hne is in front of your eyes for a little while, I mean Oh'hne the dog, then the tears will wash that away. I will be the rainbow! And trust me on this, we are all family and I am being you here."

Many words bounced about the room, but they were no longer heard. Oh'hne could not stay to keep them together. She was already gone and showing us the way to the new worlds.

Twenty

Did you grieve for Oh'hne?
I did not. With all of her being she wanted to go. I had no say in this, so it was not for me to hang on to her in any way. Oh'hne led us into the new life by going into her own world with or without our approval or needs. Even as I say this now, I do not know (nor have I attempted to know) whether or not Thomas or Marilyn knew what her dying meant to our living.

Oh'hne herself spoke simply. She told them that because they had finally released her in themselves, from themselves, unconditionally, that she was free.

My heart pounded at these words. Their meaning intensified all my being until I was not pain or joy, but knowing. Perhaps Twintreess could feel that Oh'hne was liberated. What I felt, and what I stand witness to now, is that she was the ritual. She had freed us by acting upon Thomas's and Marilyn's stated commitment. She took them at their words and she took her life into a new one. How could it be any other way, but that she also took our spirits with her?

When she jumped into all the worlds, I saw many more than seven. Perhaps that is a human translation. We joined her. A part of Ogallalah went by Oh'hne's side to each life. I, too, have forgotten none of it. I still guard her but she does not need it. I do not mind that I still need it. Spirit is served unconditionally in unlimited ways.

Marilyn and Thomas in different faces, still dance with Oh'hne in the lights. She has remained a horse. As for them, I cannot say, because that is their precious discovery. I cannot speak it for them, because I am for them.

Our lives grew and united into seasons of all our hopes. We left the home in the woods. Of course it has never left us! Since Marilyn and Thomas went there to give healing, their leaving meant that they could receive the healing back. Everywhere that we have walked since, I have seen white smoke in spirals. They are the gifts of Rocktafhar, the lake near the house. She does not leave. Her protection seems to be eternal.

One night, after leaving the northern woods, she came to me in full attire of a full moon, (thank you Oh'hne) she petted me, not with her hands but with her eyes and her hair and her belly. She breathed upon me and I flew out of my dog fur and skin. Then, we held hands. I looked just like her. Gleaming endless white. And in whatever shape brought the most comfort, we were and are of the guardian clan. Rocktafhar teaches me. It does not mean that I am less than her knowing but it means that the nature of things is for me to follow her and to give that to her so that she can leap. Same pieces of the same heart. Each one gives its blood utterly. Each one makes the world alive. I have never bowed to her.

That night, she gave me the moon. She pulled it out from her belly like an already grown and perfect child. She placed it upon my head. It was the legacy of my daughter. As I breathed it in completely I knew that I was once again giving primal breath to Oh'hne and helping her to birth a new form. Thank you Rocktafhar, you have given me the gift of myself. I have always longed to be Mother and I am still one.

Together with Thomas and Marilyn and the invisible Rocktafhar, we drove all over the country. The humans seemed to believe they had no home. I felt so at ease. Now we could have home everywhere and I was responsible for making it so. I do not apologize if there is pride in this. It is as much a part of my place in the world as being a guardian.

Every night that we stopped and camped I circled a piece of the land. I called to all the mothers of my family and I sent my breath as offering. In each moment I was prepared to give that breath in return for my family's safety. What an honor! I felt alive and I thank you all for taking in my story now as it seems to enliven me again. It reminds me that the offer is gift enough and I have given everything. That I am still alive is not a disappointment or a lesser achievement, it is simply a season that I have respected. As my breath gives these words now, I feel all those seasons closing around me, caressing me, encircling my breath. I know that my gift will soon be complete.

Twenty One

"Thank you Oh'hne. Thank you Thomas and Marilyn. Thank you Rocktafhar. Thank you clan mothers. Thank you listeners of this. We speakers and listeners come together to make one beautiful story. Where it will go is in our imagination."

Everywhere that we touched the earth, it touched us. Thomas stopped regularly, announcing to Marilyn, "There is somebody here who wants to talk to us," or "I can't drive anymore until that lake comes to us." So they would sit, sometimes, just barely off the road, sometimes we got to be in grass or in snow. Thomas always made sure that I could run and that I could mark the new territory. I would give whatever blessings were mine and they would listen to rocks, to mischievous sprites, they would listen to anything that knocked upon the door of Thomas' body. I watched over it all, telling each being to come in love. I have heard him say many times to many people, "Everything that we have ever talked to is just another form of love." I knew that already.

They grew into Twintreess. Through their roots they absorbed the timelessness of all the stories. I remember seeing Oh'hne walk by. Thomas asked, "What's that? What are you looking at?" He would laugh and go back to some fairy spinning some yarn. I sighed. I knew that Oh'hne was giving all her being and in that explosion, was like a sun that fueled their bodies so that they, Thomas and Marilyn, could reach outside of themselves without fear. She gave them fire to leap past themselves and to find others who are also adventurers who are visible, invisible, silent, loud, and loving.

In the next spring, we all went back to the north. Thomas and Marilyn had grown so many stories in their bodies, that they had to give them away to collect more. So they gathered people together and let them experience their new ancient communication. I came to almost every circle. Before they began, I sniffed out the fear that was there. I found the emotions around people that might make the stories hard to transmit. It was my place to acknowledge all of the deep emotions, even when those humans did not. All faces of loving.

Thomas and Marilyn stepped into the season of their destiny. They were spirit storygivers. The words were in Marilyn's voice and the feelings beneath them were in Thomas' body. That's why the people easily accepted Marilyn and not so easily, Thomas. Words have not always kept their meaning to all humans, but feelings do not lie. Both together are immediate power. Some people balked even at the sound of it. I watched the spirits dance. They loved it all.

Rocktafhar stood by them. Her completely focused intent made her invisible. But she visited the stories, too, and she always told them. "I give you all my unconditional love and support." The cycles of everything always returned to this. All the speaking and the sharing of stories always came back to this point and that is why it always kept coming and growing.

We continued to move about the land, staying wherever we were welcomed. Some of the beings' stories had grown into a book. They called it, "naturespeak." Now wherever we went, "naturespeak," traveled with us. Sometimes it moved down the road before us and found the places of welcome.

I followed. Even though it had not been a plan to be writers, they were carried through it by teachers of writing and they were safe.

Twenty Two

"As a guardian, it is my duty and my pleasure to tell you that you are welcome here."

Over the seasons we traveled. In some place inside of them, Thomas and Marilyn still looked for a home. Meanwhile, the spirits of everything gave them their homes. We lived freely. They got what they needed by sharing the spirit messages. It fed us and it helped us to keep looking for more family everywhere.

By listening to invisible voices, they kept coming to the desert, the southwest. They came to a place circled by mountains. They are both such mountains themselves. It was impossible for them not to be drawn there and to be taken in, in love.

More and more people from the city of mountains came to Thomas and Marilyn. They asked for guidance. They asked for hope. They asked for understanding.

Deep down, I heard them asking to be held no matter how much shame was inside of them.

So I greeted every one. I licked them, because it is my intimacy to give. Some people liked it. I answered their deepest spirits and knowing that their words, the humans words, did not always match that, I never minded if they turned me away.

Deep down a true gift is always accepted. Always. Since it is a true gift, it will serve whatever is the deepest need. And if my lick brings out feelings of uncleanliness, then that is the gift. Those feelings needed to be out of the shadows and into the air. Who am I to mind when in such a beautiful cycle of giving and receiving, if I am painted to be a dirty dog? I can see it all in a way that gives back to me. We are all true gifts.

Sometimes, people would touch me. They were loud. They laughed. They proclaimed, "Dogs just love me!"

Sorry. I am a guardian of the truth! My deepest spirit answers, "I don't feel respect in your touch. You did not ask if you could receive my gift. You assumed you could come and touch my body, just because you can. You come to take my gift, not receive it." My love is too strong for that!

One man moved the flow of the earth's seasons in my body. I warned him away because I don't feel it is respectful to change that. I honor it just as it is inside of me and in the earth. So he reached over again, knowing what was going on, but the knowing was deep, only, in his heart. He did it again. From a bellyup position, I jumped. I snapped by his hand. My being said, "I cannot allow that because life flows through me unconditionally. For you to come and try to fix it, when it is already whole, is a lie. This is my truth and I give it to you now in the snapping of my teeth."

A primal voice inside of him whispered, "Yes. This is how I am learning. My mind is trained with patterns that trace some of the flows of the universe. I place them on your body and what you gave me back was not the lines of movement but life itself. I felt it! It jumped at me! Life is not submissive to me. I am trying so hard to understand that, it is so hard. I feel hurt now. I think I am a little sad too. I still know that I am not sad or hurt by you, but by how difficult I make my lessons. You do it in a snap. I do it in a lifetime. I am that I am."

I got up quickly. I shook his symbols from my belly and I trotted to another corner of the room trying to weave past the other people talking and listening to Thomas. My voice wimpered a little because his fingers were still reaching for me. I was done with that learning and I knew he would find easier teachers than me soon.

Marilyn had seen all of it. She saw me laying before Michael, my belly up, ready to give anything, and of course ever ready to receive petting. He placed his patterns on my body. She stiffened, just at the same time I did. Our ears perked up together and our tails stopped dead still. She knew what was about to happen and watched. Sure enough, I put a stop to everything. I snapped the air by Michael's fingers, and of course being very intelligent, he drew back. Marilyn said, "She doesn't like to be touched without being asked. She is very sure of her boundaries."

I smiled. Michael was nervous, "I was adjusting her poles. I was reversing her magnetics." Finally he mumbled, "I don't know, maybe she didn't like it. I didn't think she would but...."

I leapt up because his fingers were still reaching for me and part of him still wanted to carry out the experiment. I had no need to feel like a victim.

I felt Marilyn. She had watched so she could feel

it all and wonder what exactly would she allow. Would she let someone heal her because they had decided she needed it? Would she go along because ultimately she can't be hurt? Could she learn and try saying, "No," because she had no need to be a victim? She seems to be always learning.

Twenty Three

"I have my place here, simply because it is. What is yours?"

Many beings lived with us. Some were human. Some were animal. Some had no definition They came and went through our bodies because it was our love to feel this and to share it.

There were some people who came to Thomas and Marilyn outside of groups, partly because they couldn't open their deepness to too many eyes. They came to get the answers that were in their own souls. So, Twintreess, became Twintreess, and turned to the Grandmothers and the Grandfathers of the humans before them and they would let those words flow through to find whatever meaning they needed.

I could see that Marilyn and Thomas did not always understand the messages or the other people, because they were still trying to understand those parts of themselves. I smiled. Some stories are forever. Sometimes, I have visited the people who have come to Marilyn and Thomas, believing they needed help. I came to them in words and visions so that they could be silent when they met with Twintreess. So that they could know that their gift was waiting for them. Some people have so many words bouncing inside of them, they distract themselves from the seasons of giving and receiving. They almost forget to put out their hand even though they have asked to receive.

The people who heard me, felt changed immediately. The people who didn't, felt challenged, immediately. Of course, there were full ranges of emotion all around that and in between. My visits to those asking for help accentuated the qualities that Marilyn and Thomas had. I intensified the welcoming, the ease, and the catalytic thrust. I was all of these things, too. Still am. That's why we are family. I knew that every person that came to us was also these things and part of our family and asking to remember.

Do you feel any of this, too?

Twenty Four

I love my life with my family. It would not occur to me not to do so. As a being of infinite possibilities and yet a singular focus, I celebrate all of my choices. And I have chosen to be with Thomas and Marilyn. I announce this to them with every single act. I announce it to you with these words and the complete surrender of my life story, now.

Thomas and Marilyn changed every day. They had entered the world of spiritual story-telling and forever after they could no longer be only human. I watched as they listened to beings coming and going in their days and in their night travels. Each time they explored another part of themselves. They became wolves, hawks, mountains, stars, and immortals. I could smell every new part that joined them. All my senses sharpened, but I was not alarmed. I felt that they were joining my world with theirs. We were becoming dog-humans. The equality of our souls had been acknowledged. I was free, too. Now, I was free to join them in ways that seemed unimaginable.

I went before them and I spoke to other animals of their comings. I talked to other dogs and cats and told them that they could be listened to in a new way. They could directly speak to their human families. We who have chosen to leave pieces of our wildness behind in order to walk beside people have always intended an equal partnership. We have intended to know your hearts so completely that you could not ignore ours as well.

As a guardian, I lead with alertness. I give the gifts of my family so that all of our families will grow together. Many dogs and cats heard this and in their own ways, gave the message to their humans. Soon, they in turn called Thomas and Marilyn, saying, "I have always wanted to know what my dog is saying to me. Can you help?"

Many times the animals were preparing to die and sometimes the humans were preparing to hang on to them. They all needed to listen to the season of intent and to find new ways to share their love.

It was dramatic for the people. They cried to know what the dogs were thinking. They cried when the cats said, "We are ready to go. But if you are not ready to let go, we will stay for you. We will help." It surprised them to know that animals have choices and that we act upon our choices with a ferocity of being.

When we committed ourselves to eating and sleeping and playing beside humans, we gave all that intensity and any more that came. Our piece in the grand design is to gift that. Whatever any of us is gifted with, it fills a hole in our needs. Gives us balance where we have felt missing. Perhaps humans are missing their own instincts. They are crying out for primal love and passion in every step.

Ogallalah de Oro 77

If that is you, it is extended to you now.

Twenty Five

I sleep as often as I wish. I can awaken completely whenever I need to do so, because I sleep not to escape the myriad sights and sounds of the world. I delve into other worlds where my soul is welcomed, time and again.

So I experience a twin existence as well. I live here with Twintreess and I journey with other parts of them in dreamwalks. Everything is sharp and full there. Nothing is distant or avoided. I have guarded them awake and asleep. I have watched them travel the country and many dimensions simultaneously. It is that simple when you decide.

They formed many partnerships with lots of spirits. I hardly watched those. They lay like a natural bond between them and the others. I watched more the alliances with humans because I could feel hurt coming on. I told them in little ways, so as not to disturb their choices. I chased the cats of one of their printer friends. I let them see the nervousness tingling on my back. I stayed away from some of the meetings with those humans that said, "Yes, yes! We want to explore everything," while their bellies cried, "We are afraid." I laid in the corners and sent the fear past us. But I did not ask them, any of them, to stop.

In the dream worlds, Thomas and Marilyn and I talked all of it over. Especially Thomas. He has always liked to have me nearby while he sleeps. We roll over together and slip out of our skins and roam the land. He came to me one night. The new moon was across his shoulders. His wings shadowed the light. His eyes moved like a hawk's. Sometimes we have rolled in fields and got grass in our hair/fur. We would run and skip all over rocks, but tonight the fun crystallized. It hung in the air with all seriousness and unlimited respect. We climbed a mountain, not by walking, but by being the mountain. It stood with us as witness.

"I am not very much human," Thomas began. "That body is tired and needs to rest with the earth for a while. I be here with you now so I can cherish my wings and my fur and every instinct possible. You have helped me even when I have not wanted help. You have pushed the feelings that I had about the world, out in frustration, so I could keep freeing myself. What can I do now? I would like to know other humans who touch the earth like this. I would like to feel them roam freely in my life and to take all of my gifts however they wish. And I would like to truly know them. I am ready to have a human family, too."

I looked right through him into time. We could see everything from this mountain. The rivers of choice lay very clearly. I see where you befriended a woman who is now leaving your side. There is sadness so that you can leave a space for what is next. Yes. I smell others coming. They have hunted for us, too. They seem lonely in the world but very willing. Out of all the voices that come to you, these two voices will find you. They already love you and you them. Our bodies go to them tomorrow."

    He sighed. He had seen this road of the future, but no one could translate it to his human body but him. So we laid upon the mountain rocks. They softened beneath us. We buried all our feelings there for a moment. A hundred suns filled the sky. They rose and fell in our amusement. Nothing else mattered.

Twenty Six

The next morning, we went to Brad's and Anna's house. Thomas and Marilyn were giving them a reading and Brad and Anna were giving their selves.

I got to go right in while they kept their dog in the backyard. I was admired immediately, so it was a good deal for me. I went to sleep so that I could talk to the fairies sliding down the roof and bouncing off the plants.

I could have listened to the reading but I had already heard everything in my veins the night before. Before we left, Brad and Anna offered their house as a space to have gatherings of spirit-talking as often as possible.

Our new family had found us.

Twenty Seven

Adventures came from everywhere. I felt Thomas and Marilyn crawling out of the woods and into the city. I knew their bodies were searching for the sacredness under the cement and the concrete that they felt in the tree roots in the far away from people places.

Brad and Anna were the bridge between the worlds. Our contract with knowing everything and everybody, including people and all their sacredness, was spiraling through us into timelessness.

Even when I was awake, little spirits walked up to me and whispered in my ear, "They are going to be giving their stories to everybody. We've put all our hope into this, and we are stretching these stories around the world."

I watched as the astral bodies, the light bodies, of many humans visited all of us at Brad and Anna's house. They changed, they changed the ethers in the rooms. They smoked their prayers to the heavens. They cast circles of welcome. They were welcoming themselves into our lives.

I took note of all of it. One day Thomas and Marilyn drove us to the ocean. White spirals of Rocktafhar wrapped around us. And while Twintreess was working by the Mexican ocean, I was working, too. I laid bridges between them and the heart of Rocktafhar that lay open on the beach for them to remember. The water has always seeped into their being magically. It moves through them and it soothes them beyond understanding. Rocktafhar spoke to them every day by the ocean, but left no traces of words. When they came back home, the sea vibrated in their veins. They were more themselves and they gave it all to Brad and Anna and a new partnership. Our family grew into a circle around the whole earth.

Twenty Eight

From the day that they formed TreeHouse Press, my mission soared. As I lay back in the feeling of it, it is comfortable. We have always known each other. Whispers from its heart to mine have carried me through many bodies. It brings me to now and everything is sharp, clear, and extremely precious.

I am Ogallalah de Oro. In human time, I picked that name recently and I came to a woman who sang spirit songs with her voice and her piano. I nudged her and she told Thomas and Marilyn my secret name. Actually, she said, "She has a new name. I think it's Ogallallallalllahhhhsomething." I wagged my tail and she found the movement in it. That was about a year ago. The same time that Brad and Anna and we met for what seemed the first time.

Along the way, I slipped the rest of my name to them. Ogallalah de Oro. It vibrates to Golden Books of

Truth. That's how it pulses in my body. I give it to my family as a reminder that they will always write from their truth. Stories are not made up, they are lived. And then they are given away. Everyone else adds a piece. It becomes the sky with a million stars.

That's why I came into this life story. I have walked around in it. It nuzzles me like a good old friend. If there have been hard moments, they have not stayed hard in my feelings. They have melted away and become songs somewhere else. With my spirit I thank all the beings who have crossed my path.

Most of you remain nameless here and that is your power. To Thomas, I say, "Hello, again. Our hearts keep meeting and words between us are forever. We have pledged ourselves to each other in sacred rings of fire. We have visited stars from the sky. You have forgotten some, because that is your task. I have forgotten none, because that is my task. Sometimes the places around us have seemed strange and we have learned to nest our bodies in many new smells and colors. Inside my dreams I see that we find indescribable places to be. How amazing that we don't lose the family of us in all of it! The blood lines between us travel anywhere. My bones feel a little tired now and my spirit grows sharper. I travel in the dreamtime constantly and I am saving many adventures for you. I don't expect you to record them all but I imagine you will live them all."

To both of you, "We move together in a new land, a new bond. My guardianship withers away. You have links to everything and your need for my intercession dwindles. I like that. The talk of a hundred beings pounds in my chest and it is there for me so I can give it away to everyone. I am not sure this body has ever felt this free! But how would I know? I don't measure freedom. I have learned much and I love even more."

"I feel family from everywhere, swooping down to join us! They have many gifts, as do we. The time to call out loud, 'All beings are free and equal,' is now. I give all my life to sound that right here, this moment."

Twenty Nine

None of this will seem to fit here but it is my life and I have to give it as it is. I danced inside the full moon last night. All the elders smiled at me. But they did not extend a hand. Their faces were mountains and they made the circle of time. I gave my life and breath to the circle. It was an earth offering to a water being.

In another story, he was from my body. He was powerful, and for a moment, he allowed himself to be my son. When the moon was right over the top of me, I gave her my song. The tones came from my heart, my belly, and from the shaking of my fur. They are all that I know how to give. She pulled them in like the tide. Every gift, every breath, she absorbed and when it was done, she smiled. The echo rang across the world. There were no other noises. My holy songs smiled all the way around the world and they landed in the heart of this being who does not live beside me, but still lives inside of me.

As a creature of the sea, he drank in the music I had made for him, the music that described his life with me, the music that honored his fur, his large head, and a pink star on his nose. I felt him smile all over me. I cannot tell you that he remembers, but I feel he never forgets.

He rolled in the salt water as he listened and he gave me paddling and bouncing in the waves. He gave me a flick of his tail, that sent a shower of salt air. The bonds of family hold us and spin us and they set us free. I honored his time with me and I honor it, now. And the celebration showers me in life. I have sent him all of my story so that he can write it along side of his and our lives are as big as the moon and the stars.

My worship of family is forever. But for you listening, I have placed it in your time. I have danced the ritual dance on the anniversary of his birth.

He is birthed again and again.

Thirty

"Everything circles and circles around us until there is nothing left unjoined. We create no loneliness today."

Marilyn rolled and rolled in the bed under the full moon. Its grin was wrapped around its head, full of teeth, "Come and play. Come and play, now!"

She smiled inside knowing that it could be seen. She remembered the ease and then lifted freely. She floated just above her body to make sure that it was calm. She swayed back and forth, keeping the heart together. Then she stood outside her home and laughed inside and outside at the moon. The full moon always knows when there's more of you that has to come out.

She walked in the sands, waiting, but it was a gentle wait. It didn't push her and it didn't need anything. It already knew the hour of arrival. Marilyn looked up.

From behind the mountain above her, a pink glow rose. It didn't compete with the moon; rather, the moon drew it out until a being appeared.

It was a white horse. It floated down the mountain to Marilyn. They stood facing each other. If you could see them, it would look as if they were standing a little ways apart completely still. But if you looked through them, past beliefs, and if you kept peering through the dimensions to the next and the next, you could watch their arms unfold, then their legs. They unstretched their limbs and it became a dance. It was a dance of welcome. Then the dance became a hug. Through a few more dimensions, they held each other all over. Then, past time, they released each other and sighed out everything. The release became silence. It was a void between them and through them, dancing with only stillness.

Look again. You might see they had never moved and that they were still standing and facing each other, naked in the desert sand and under a full moon.

I watched it all, or whatever part the spirits gave me eyes to see. They met this way often. They had met exactly like this so often, that there was no need to hold onto a memory. For Marilyn, it lingered in her body so constantly that she could not miss it, she could only experience it over and over again. There was a part of her, probably her spirit, that knew it, that knew it all. That was why it had rocked her body to sleep before she had gone out to be with the white horse. Her spirit gave her body comfort and cellular memory so that traveling to and from could be easy.

The white horse looked familiar. It was tall, but not unearthly tall. It seemed to be old, but it didn't hold age inside of it. Most of all, it breathed and it spoke easily. Everything between her and Marilyn was simple and uncomplicated ...

By plans or feelings, they floated to the edge of their little cliff, not because they needed to sit down somewhere, but because it seemed comfortable to do so. It gave understanding and acknowledgement to the earth part of their being. So the two of them sat on the stones, drinking in the moon and remembering that they had always been together.

The horse touched Marilyn. Its touch on her body was not exactly like a hoof. It was warm. She could feel that there was blood inside of it. The horse stroked her quietly. Everything hushed. Everything leaned to listen and to nod.

"I feel alone," Marilyn uttered. "I feel alone and I still feel you right now. I feel your touch as much as I feel everything in the world. When I wake up in the morning, I won't remember how to feel this."

The cactus, the stones, the stars, the moon, all sighed. Everything in the desert night breathed together. Some were fragrant, some were not. Each listened and nodded in their own way. The horse stared at Marilyn. No eyes blinked. Words finally formed from the length of their eyes meeting.

The horse said, "I always meet with you. I come to you by night just as you have asked. I have seen you grow and I have walked by when you have wanted somebody else for company. You know this. You know that I am with you forever. You can see me anytime. You can touch me any way. Whatever form pleases you, we will find it together. We always have. I picked this horse shape tonight right out of a page of your life. I grabbed it from a little girl of eight who collected ceramic horses. Nobody knew why! Even she/you, didn't know why, but you kept collecting them. When your mother asked if that meant you wanted to ride a horse, you said no. Then you stopped collecting them, because you couldn't imagine what they were for."

The horse grinned just like the moon. "That's when you started collecting rocks. Did you ask for the toy horses because you could remember me from now, from this moment in the desert when you pretend to be grown up in a dream, or were you trying to call me? I have finally come. It is all the same. With the seasons, the tail of one is held in mouth of the head of the next. The beginnings and endings are wrapped in each other. When you unravel them everything comes apart and everything comes to you, except maybe making sense of it."

Marilyn touched the tip of the nose of the horse. She glowed. They both glowed from head to tail. Marilyn spoke, "I just have to experience all of it, all together. When I pull out one piece it is just one piece. It can speak for the whole if I let it, because that's where we all are from."

"My whole body just sighed. I am very glad that you give me these moments. I know I am learning and it is not the learning that I remember in my body that makes me feel incomplete. I am already complete and that means that I will always stretch out. I keep growing because I have chosen this. If I forget in my human body, it is because I have chosen this and I learn this, too. I feel that in my bones, and it never goes away, but it doesn't have these words. It doesn't reflect to me the way that it does right now, the way that your eyes give it to me, here."

They stared into each other. They looked very still. The horse grew. She changed. She molded a shape from the air. Her back straightened. Her mane almost touched the ground and her tail fluffed out and held itself high up into the air. The horse was red all over. A full red, holding the rise of the sun in her body, just waiting to spill onto the world.

She reached out and she touched Marilyn's forehead. Heat shimmered off the touch. Then they both flew over the mountains. They raced down the hills whenever they wanted to feel legs again. They sat on big rocks and looked for night animals. They laughed at the city in the distance and waved to all the ancestors in the skies. I believe they are still playing in the canyon right now. If you hurry you can ride with them.

Thirty One

"One story blesses the next, and the next. That is not time, that is forever."

A full moon breeds restlessness, especially in certain hearts. Tonight, everything moves around our little home. In the distance, a bobcat hunts sleeping birds. Noises of all kinds raise to exactly certain pitches. They form a hum that weaves a song, and somebody smells it. The tree just outside the window scratches on the door, "Come out. Come out and play, now."

Thomas taps the tree from behind and smiles, "I am already out. I am always out looking for adventure."

The tree stiffened. Its roots trembled and its branches shook. Its blackness seeped away until silver hair shone. Two blue eyes popped out. Then two arms, two legs, a body, came from the trunk. The face looked lined. It was just as wrinkled as it should be. She was a serious Grandmother. She was always ready for work. She smiled at the trailer home and that was her blessing as she climbed up the mountain with Thomas.

They seemed silent. Each toe dug into the earth and sent a sprinkle of stones downward. They crawled on ledges. They pushed themselves past cactus. They lifted tree branches so that they could hold those hands before they passed by. Every movement was a word. Every touch of the earth was a thought they left behind. They kept climbing and bit by bit they knew more. They heard each other's silence and they understood. They liked breathing hard as they inched to the mountaintop, all the while knowing that they could have flown through everything and simply landed there.

At the top, they paused. They were surrounded by peaks who were accustomed to these two nightly visitors. But they stopped in gratitude for what they had done. The Grandmother pulled out a pipe from her heart. It was very, very long. It shone like crystal in the moon's glance. She drew upon it consciously, perfectly, and then she smoked her prayer to the cloudless sky. This would go right to the heart of the creator. Nothing in between. Each puff slid through her. It was an art. She shaped and kneaded each piece of smoke like a new being that she had just met and loved infinitely. All her being became the smoke. She sighed in and wooshed out. The flow laced the air in a language that Thomas could smell. He became the song of that pipe. He shaped himself to each breath. He smoked himself to the heavens. He understood and he did not care.

This is how they greeted the dawn. He turned to the Grandmother and spoke aloud, "I have to go back to my day."

Thirty Two

"Now." I am laying outside in the desert. Thomas is writing. Marilyn is speaking. I burrow my body into the sand. There is a tree for company and a ring of Moqui stones lays with me. Their touch is utter gentleness. They draw out of me easy breaths. Do I remember them? I don't know. But they seem to remember me.

My body feels a little sore, like it's been very busy doing something else while I sleep here. My heart is bigger. It pounds more. Of course, that means something and, of course, I will wait till it tells me what. For now, I talk to Thomas and Marilyn. It just comes out of me. I suppose that it has to so that they will grow and feel more complete. It is not easy for me. Does this mean that you will think that it is hard? I often feel humans listening to words so that they can jump to the opposite meanings. I did not say it was hard for me to talk like this.

This kind of speaking rolls around inside of me and it moves itself while it moves my body. It keeps me alert even while I sleep. It tells me when flies zoom by my face ... It opens my heart so that Twintreess can walk through me whenever they want.

So I talk like this all the time. It is my life. What you are reading right now is not easy. For me to translate this into a humanness, that is easy for you, makes me stretch my limbs and pound my heart. I turn myself inside out and whatever is there falls into your language. It's like diving into a river and pushing yourself farther and farther into it, knowing that if you turned around now you still wouldn't make it to the surface. You are starved for air and you still push yourself from something, I don't know what it is. Maybe the water wills you deeper in. It's so deep that it is silent and it is dark. Then you know you have nothing left. All you can do is burst. Your lungs burst, your heart sprays open. Your mouth gulps. You can't stop yourself and you know you are dying. You are dying because there is nothing else left. And as the water rushes in, you realize that it has air inside. The air inside slips out and it finds your exploded lungs and heart. It pulls them together, but they are bigger then they were (your lungs and your heart, that is.). Air is so sweet. Right then it's like your very best friend. It rewards you for everything you've done. It thanks you. It exalts you. It blesses you through and through. And when it leaves, it's a story. The story swims through the water hidden inside of it just like it was before. And it floats to the top where everything began. It lays like a bubble on the surface. It's all colors and it is achingly fragile.

Marilyn sighs it. Tosses it around in her breath and it becomes a different voice. Thomas scoops the bubbles into his hand. I don't think he's ever broken one.

When everything bursts, it's clear. The air talks

to you and tells you the story that's carried. This time it's my story.

That's what I mean by not easy. I talk to me constantly, but I don't put that into words. Usually. This is what I'm learning. Giving this story stretches me a piece at a time. I feel the rhythm and the pounding of it. There is no turning back (not that I want to). It's another piece of me coming out. I think it's partly the moon! I know it's partly an invisible water being pulling me along. I'm going nowhere that I can see, but I move just as quickly. I put alertness in every step.

Here it comes out as a word or two. I travel this way a lot. I gave up on understanding, not that I don't believe in it, but it doesn't seem to need my belief to be.

I decided, yesterday, today, and tomorrow, to be with Thomas and Marilyn. Especially Thomas [no favorites. He asked first.]. They change every second. To be with them, I have to change or die. Sometimes I have died.

They live at the surface of the water where it meets the air. The air is easy for them. It bounces off them. It makes shapes. It giggles. It tickles them and they hardly know that air could be hard for someone else. Marilyn and Thomas come together in the air. I watch it. They move towards each other even when they are not facing each other. The air spirals around. Colors are everywhere. Little words drop from the skies like presents. It's that easy. They scoop them up and when they put them on paper, they're stories from fairies.

The stories became a book, and no matter what Marilyn and Thomas called it, I recognize it. It's the book of life. They open it over and over again Thomas runs his finger down the pages in a single sweep. He goes through it one page at a time, hoping he will find the one word that he can use to give to other humans so that they will understand. He needs for somebody to understand him in a single word. Can you imagine?

He told me the other day while he was petting me, that he was just about ready to give up the search. And it dawned on him that maybe he could stop trying to translate himself into human. He's realizing, in his book of life, that lots of beings are reading him and understanding perfectly. Actually there are unlimited beings doing that. Most of them don't seem to be human right now, that's all. That's why Thomas is writing this right now. He's learning how to read, to speak, and to understand human. This will make you laugh: I am helping!

Anyway, as you have already heard, Thomas and Marilyn come together so that they can put their breath into lots of different stories and languages and then translate them into human. They've traveled a lot and they've talked to trees. They've talked to mountains that have given them a home so they can practice stillness. They've talked to a rattlesnake that they walked right by so that they could know that they didn't have to be hurt. They've talked to stones that they live with so that they could know that everything has life, every shape chooses that life, and if you listen past yourself, that rock or that shape has a story just a little bit different from the rest. I have been with Marilyn and Thomas before, during, and after, all these conversations. I have listened with them. I personally greet all the beings who come to them. I give their spirits a home for as long as they want. Though I'm not sure Marilyn and Thomas know this exactly, I give all the other lives inside of them places to be. I give them houses to rest in. When I am asleep, I give them this story so they can stretch themselves. When they are asleep I come as the Grandmother, or whatever they want and I mother them. That's easy for me. I mother them no matter who they are.

Remember when Thomas and I climbed the mountain? He asked for that. He willed his spirit to climb even though he didn't need to do it. He chose that so he could break open the shell of his body and leave it empty in the moonlight. Thomas forced himself into a new world so he could feel a new Thomas. Just like me swimming deep inside of myself until I burst and cough up these words.

He and I meet in those places where hard and easy are the point, they are the tip of the mountain. When we are there, I hold him in intent, in freedom, knowing we will make human sentences from them whenever he needs. I love him just the way he is.

I have told you already that Thomas and Marilyn live by speaking like this. They push and pull themselves out of shape and find new ones. They pour these words into books, into tapes, into a whole new way of life where this is how they support themselves and how they support the world as they choose to see it.

I have been with them when they have let the stories of other beings slip through their voices and they have given them to groups of people. The people come whether they understand or not, looking for wisdom. I sniff each one. They are just the same. They are not looking for something outside of themselves (even when they speak to other stars.). I feel them trying to pull the wisdom from deep inside of themselves. They struggle to remember out loud the last time they touched life.

This is also why I travel with Twintreess. I go to meet every human they meet. I feel them reaching out to my heart and asking about my guardianship. I have seen men and women sit in circles and tell Marilyn about their work and about their fun. Beneath that, their spirit glows.

Sometimes it lays next to me and we speak different language. It asks me, "Who are you? Why do you be a guardian? Will you protect me? Who is in the universe and wants to know me? Where do I come from and where do I go?"

I record it. I nod because they are not asking for answers. Those they will try to get from other humans. I nod because I want to be with them and I am with them. That is my choice. I give them whatever comfort they can receive. I give it to you right now because you are asking for it. You are asking to know that there is more to life than a single human body.

Thirty Three

"When I look at the big world and I feel scared, my Grandmother comes to me and says, 'That's inside of you.'"

When Marilyn and Thomas first started collecting stories, it was easy as air. They breathed them in and out and it was exciting. They caught on to the rhythm and they danced in it. They knew the steps even before the music began and they thought that a lot of the steps would be the same from person to person or from being to being.

Life loves a surprise.

The way that Thomas and Marilyn listened to spirits and recorded them, is changing. It's changing because their own ears are changing. It's changing because their hearts are a new color. They have begun to dive into the air and they've had to push it through them even when they have felt sad or alone. The stories carried them when they couldn't carry themselves.

So I have come today to talk as a piece of those stories and tell Thomas and Marilyn the part that has come to speak of them.

"Hello, Marilyn and Thomas. Hello, Twintreess. We are the circles of your clan. We are your cousins in other lives. We have been casting out our thoughts to catch your curiosity. Your ears are growing and you have found snippets of conversations that you couldn't hear before. This is different from talking to the beings who walk with you every day. It's different because you have decided that it is and we honor that. So come and find us. We are in corners that when you get to them, they explode and we become universes for you to travel inside. If you are going to talk to your outer reaches, you will travel blind. You will come alone but you will find everything that you need. Come to us. We already see you here."

That's the message that has been beaming through my body. I play it to you, Thomas and Marilyn, because you have been too busy to receive it. Your bodies are tired because you have not let them breathe the next explosion. At the same time, you are already doing this and much more. I am here. I am with you and I am your guardian.

Bye.

Thirty Four

"Why are we together like this?"

I have come to be with you because I can teach you and you can teach me. If you're curious at all, then your being here springs from that need to learn, too. So, there are our essences, naked in front of us. We can talk, we can do anything and we can go right now to the reason why we are here.

Let me teach you. Sit down. Move until you find the exact spot where your spine will support you evenly and smoothly. Then, when you're sitting in that spot, let everything else just fall from your back. Your arms and legs can hang or you can hold them. Let your head be gentle on top of your neck. Sit completely still. Let the distractions pass through you. Be focused now on what I have to say. When your body is balanced and completely quiet, you can hear everything else. You can hear now not only with your ears but with the bottoms of your feet. Hear with your legs. Hear with your heartbeat. Hear from the roots to the tips of your hair. Don't move unless it is that your body has shifted out of its balanced spine place. Then go ahead and move. Erect yourself perfectly and let stillness follow. Your breathing is natural and absolutely follows the rhythm that is inherent in these words. They have been designed for this. They are for you and you can have them all. Or you can have as little as you want. The richness of everything is up to you.

Breathe up and down your spine, but don't count, don't measure the length. Your breath is holding your spine in space. The space and your spine hold your body together. It is natural. If you feel discomfort, then let it pass through bit by bit. All of your organs, your muscles, and your nerves unfold themselves. They release themselves from being whatever you imagine them to be. They lay open in the wind of your breath. They are free. Every point in your body surges and drops with your single breath and with my single word. Breathe. You are a unit. You are an organized flow of your body and your being. As each moment comes to you, you connect it to your breath, which connects it to you, as a whole. You are a single breath, you are a single organ, you are a single being.

Now sit exactly like this, still and full of yourself for one hour. Read this over if you wish. Read it until your breath enters the words and you create them. Do this many times. Your whole being is relaxed and it is alert. So is mine. This is how my body lives.

You have learned this from my body.

Thirty Five

"The teaching has just begun."

There. I have just given you a human lesson. Why? Because you are human (Some of you.). And you have habits that respond readily to that kind of learning. What that means is that you are practiced at having someone or something tell you what to do and keeping your mind busy, so that you won't go past the learning at hand. I gave you an exercise that would fill up your thinking and take away your questions, if that's what you wanted. Those of you with questions, keep bringing them. I busied your mind and most of you like that. You like that even when you don't like the words I used or the way I said them. It still occupies you. It keeps you in your habits and the space around you stays familiar.

Well, does this fit you or doesn't it?

You decide that for yourself, even when you think that you don't. I'm not going to tell you how to sit anymore. I'm glad that I did it this once because it's something I have learned from you. I have watched humans all my life. I let their thoughts run through me and I see where I can go to because of them.

Your thoughts run me from one thing to the next to the next, instantly. It's exciting. It's draining. And it reminds me that I am a dog learning from you. I feel all that you are and then I give it back to you so you can see how you look and so you can feel yourself without the same distractions. As a dog who has decided to live with people, I have chosen to teach and to study by reflecting back to you all of your thoughts. This probably seems like a lot, but it is what you give me. When it is too much, I choose to go away and to lay in my own circle and to know myself. It doesn't mean I don't love you. It means I am me.

If you follow me and make me take all your thinking, or if you follow me to give me what you think I need from a human place, I will not accept. I will give it back to you and you decide what kind of a gift it is. You decide if you have given me an exercise telling me how to be. You decide what it feels like to try and make somebody be you. It won't work with me, because I am free.

Thirty Six

"The learning has just begun."

What I have to give you is my dog-ness. It permeates everything until there is only this: It is. I am not confident or insecure because I am myself. If you want to come with me, crawl inside of me. I won't tell you that there is only one way because you'll make up your own way of coming to me. You'll learn just as much as you can give yourself. I am already giving everything.

Let's be dogs. If you think about this then you'll be a human trying to be a dog. Just come with me. Come quickly. Come before you can decide anything. Jump into it. Lay down beside me. Nestle up in the dirt. This is my home. I move and I shape the ground until it soothes me, until my bodies can lay on smooth bones. I let it hold me. I let the earth hold me because it's there.

Let's lay into the wind. The smells of anything we need to know will come at us whenever we need them.

Besides, the wind ruffles my fur and deep down my skin is cooled. It is heated and itchy from shedding all my winter coat.

Stretch out every part of your body. You can have as much or as little space as you want. My head is in the dirt. It feels like family. It smells like spring coming. There are green things whose hearts are beating just below the surface. They are coming up to meet me. I don't know when. They will tell me every time I sleep on the ground. When they come up, it will be spring and I will eat the grasses when they ask me to do so. My body will clean itself for a new season. I feel it already shifting its movements and its pulses. It grows into the sun. I will take what I need from the sun coming into my body. I will make less heat with my blood. Even more of my coat will drop into the desert and fly away.

We're asleep and all that you have just seen is my dream. I dream of the seasons in my body. They tell me what I will need to know. They caress me and I feel love. When I awaken, the dream goes on in my chest, my heart. It perks up my ears. It runs through my legs. It keeps my senses alive so I will know how to protect my truth. I will know how to guardian with my family. This is how I learn. Whatever is asked of me will be given so that I can give it and then I eat from the same plate. I walk in the world full of instincts. They draw themselves ready to spring.

At exactly the right pitch or smell, I move, completely ready. I don't understand how or when because it is given to me by the sun, the wind, the earth, and by my choices. I don't remember my choices because I am them. If you want to know them, if you want to list them, then keep walking with me. They jump out all of the time. They are simply me. My choices mate with my instincts. They are the same blood inside of me. They drive me and I drive them. As I feel, I act. I act with all the power stored in my body. I have no pride or shame about this. That is something I have learned from humans, so I know of those feelings, but I have not kept them.

I lay in the grass and in the rocks. I lay with such completeness, that whatever feelings you give me tremble through me now and they seep into the earth. If I need some of those feelings to give to another, they will stay inside my bones for awhile, and when they tell me the moment is ripe for giving them to another, I do it.

Come back into the nest we have made in the dirt. Shake your skin and your hair out first. Then you can feel fire in the air and the water inside the earth. Everything is everywhere at once. You are such consciousness. You can come now and bring everything and be nothing with me. Lay down, lay your heart inside of mine. Watch me. Your whole body stops, except your eyes. Drink me in. I am black and white fur burrowed into the earth. I have surrendered myself over completely to this half-sleep.

Watch me. Model yourself. Shape yourself like a dog. Look at my belly. It shakes with every breath and when I exhale it goes out in a sigh. Let it be your belly. My skin and fur touch the earth and she talks to me. She talks through me. Feel the earth touching you. Don't let your feelings stop at your own skin. Reach past them so that you can feel the earth yielding to your body and rocking it. She is smooth and she is cool and she is still our family. Whatever secrets she tells you, they will come out your pores with sweat and breath. This is what feeds all the life. Whatever we need will stay with our body until it is time to go.

Can you watch me some more? My body is always ready. It is ready to move. It is ready to sleep. It is ready for both of these, equally. It's in our breath.

Don't watch anymore. Be it. Be ready to be whatever the earth asks of you. You are choosing now.

Thirty Seven

"I am learning human."

Do you want to know more? I am ready.

Inside of this dream, my heart lies open at your hand. Do it. Reach in. Touch it. Feel it, for as long as you want. I give it to you. It is old but it is not less than it was. It is touching you now. My heart speaks. Pull out whatever form you will understand. Pull out the vision that you will recognize.

Look again. I appear before you. I am new. My dog body will watch over the spots on the earth where we lay, relaxed and empty. I walk out and about in wonder as the Grandmother. See that as you will. Let it be a face from your family, if that's what you need. In my barest essence, I take all that I am and I fire it so that it will spark your soul. My core gives itself absolutely, completely, over and over again. Those are the seasons of my being. It is always time for me to give away my essence. If that shapes itself as a lick or a growl, it will be you who is sculpting it.

    I am utter essence. I know this completely. I can never leave it beside me. It sings in my breath. It wags my tail, and it presents me countless bodies in which to visit and to dream. That is how I come to you now. In one of the bodies that springs from the passion of my dog-ness. The Ogallalah in me allows me the readiness to wear the form that helps you to see me now.

    Feel free. Be free. You are as free as you can design freedom. Look upon me. This face comes from your thoughts. Its edges and colors are from your choices. Touch me. I am as real as you and I am ready to be embraced by you. I have come past time and places, just to be with you now. I want to know you. I already love you. I asked to feel even more of you. Your being is powerful. It is clear and it is cloudy and it is sharp to my dog body. I choose to listen to it constantly. I choose to place my learning with yours.

    Know this from Ogallalah and the Grandmother before you: I choose to be me. My learning from you is complete, but I will not be you. It is not possible, so I will not try. I keep my instincts sharp and my freedom unlimited. As a Grandmother, I hold your hand and tell you I do not create human feelings. I do not own dis-ease, shame, pride. I think of nothing. This is who I am. I live next to the void, but I do not know it. We are companions who ask nothing particular of each other. We flow through each other and carry a piece of that ALL, in walks upon the earth.

    If you truly ask to learn from me, then watch my every movement. All my essence lies inside the smallest act. I focus my being in everything. I don't offer success or failure, I offer myself. Sit with me. Run with me. Let your body imitate mine. Pant like me. See what it is in the

distance that has perked up my ears and holds my gaze for long moments. If you witness me then you feel my essence coming to your movements.
    I go back to my sleep, now.
    Goodbye.

Thirty Eight

It's nighttime on the mountain, and Thomas and Marilyn are asleep. I'm lying outside. The air is buzzing with life. I look at the stars and they reach down to me and walk circles around our home. I know that she is coming, so I'll wait here with our star friends. I'm both asleep and awake and I feel a glow travel up and down my back. It finds my sore spots and coos at them. I am a little baby in the night, in the stars, and in this glow, that grows until it faces me. We look through each other. We look and we look. Then I reach out and I take its hand, because I can see that it is younger than me. I teach it to walk a little ways up the mountain, one thought at a time. Without looking, I know that it is sniffing the mountain lion in the air and feeling the cool stones beneath its feet. I point us towards the top of the mountain, and there it is. The moon is hanging just at the top. For one night, the mountain holds it up in the sky so she can rest, and I can see the patience and the giving in her power. I bow. I turn to the glow beside me. It is Marilyn. And it is time.

"The moon has come to be with us. She is shining right into our souls. We must stand very clearly so that we can feel the honor of her pass right through us. My mother taught me to do this. You stand here until everything in you gives way. You crumble like a piece of sandstone, except that we are crumbling from the inside out when the moon turns to stare at us. She will look right through us. She is reminding us that we are reminding ourselves that we are invisible."

I look at Marilyn without turning my head. I know she is feeling with wonder. Her face whitens like a child's. All wrinkles and cares have been smoothed by the moon's touch. We both look like two comets, stars with endless tails. Nothing in us is stopping the light. With no words, we lay down side by side, holding each other.

Marilyn says, "This feels like forever. I don't need to talk, but I am amazed that I can. We have joined with the moon and I feel all things female. I am missing nothing."

I sigh, just because my body wants it. "It is your moon-time. We have always done this in your moon-time. We have felt the earth bleeding as it twists and it turns, so we come out here to bleed a little upon her, to let her know that we are with her. I know that she does not need us and I know that she does not need this, but everything in my being wants to give it, so I do not question it. And I know these drops of life that we leave here are for someone. They are for something. Whoever it is, they do not need my answers."

We lay there and find no words to call out our feelings, but we are deeply embraced in love. Every time she shivers, I feel a new wave of us going into the earth and into the moon and into the holy blood. I do not search out my feelings, but I am satisfied beyond my body. I am satisfied beyond my will. I am content.

Bit by bit, I see pictures walk in the sky above us. I see Marilyn in younger faces going out into the night with me, and sometimes with others. I smile at the scene where she is running with the red horse – truly Oh'hne means infinity. I'm glad she has had someone to play with her. It is not my job. I am guardian. My teachings are of mystery and buried truths finding us.

I can feel something in the air. It is already touching me but I know that it is not present yet. It smells like ginger. I know who it is and my body sighs to make room for welcome.

Thirty Nine

Thomas. It is Thomas, coming to lay with us. I do not have to make more room because he is already here. His glow goes right through us and mingles with the moon. Marilyn sighs, too.

Then he opens up his truth and he is singing. He sings through the mountain. He sings pyramids around the moon. He sings to the stones holding all of us up to the sky. He sings his tears at being here again. There are no human words. The voice is primal. It leaves an emptied throat and heart. It just gives itself over and over. It sounds like a wolf howl.

I begin to tremble and sweat into the wind. My furs stand higher than my body, reaching out to a new hand. Somebody else is coming to our family. Somebody is coming. It echoes in the canyon like a drum, and I am excited beyond myself, but I do not understand just yet. I don't need to understand yet. I need to be here with

Thomas and Marilyn. My job is to lay out the welcome from all of us.

So I wake up. I bark and I howl so that I can feel the vitality of my body. I paw at the two of them and I see the glow drip from them into the earth. It is an offering.

They turn and they look at each other. Marilyn laughs, "We did it. We did it! We brought ourselves into our dream world. Look," she points at Thomas, "our bodies are with us." He stares at us both and at his hands and I can hear his thoughts, "The same, but not exactly the same. We are here, but we are a little different."

Marilyn hugs me to see if she can. And her laugh is still very loud. "You've been bringing us together into this for a long time."

I know that part of her meant that as a question, but as soon as she started to say it, the truth slipped right out.

Then we sat on the rocky dirt and arranged ourselves away from the stickers and formed a circle. As soon as we did that, the glow wrapped around us and a hum connected our bodies. It rose and rose until my ears started to scream, "It's too high for my ears!"

I sighed deeper than ever making the welcome around me deeper and sure. Ogallalah, the dog, became Ogallalah, the storyteller, right before them. When I looked into Thomas' and Marilyn's eyes, I could see my reflection. I had long silver hair and a human face. On my back was a buffalo robe. I settled deeper into my body and I could feel the being that I was becoming. I was the Grandmother again. They wished for me and their wishes made it so.

I sat cross-legged and motioned for them to do the same so that our knees would touch. Then I prayed, "Hello Grandmother Moon. We sit beneath your watchful eye again, and just like you, we change our face, over and over. You have given us the magic to step into new bodies and to remember ourselves. My stories come from you. I am telling them to these, sometimes human, ones. They are putting them on paper and making sense of them. We offer them to you. We offer all our wisdom to you and to our spirits that stand high in the sky and to the earth with you. Any wisdom that passes through us will be as free as your moonbeams. I give you all our gratitude."

    I bowed my face into the earth and I could still see the white light of the moon. Thomas said to me, "Ogallalah, help us. Help us to remember this. Can you help us to put this into our humanness so that we can record it for others? We want to put it into words for all the others who don't hear you right now." I looked at him and he was crying. "Some of them are sleeping right now, just like parts of me are sleeping. I want with my whole spirit to be awake. If I give that to everyone, then I give that to myself. I want to be so alive with everything that we do and everything that you give us."

    Grandmother-me answered, "I am still a dog, too. I will not remember this in words. I will remember this by need. If you need it then I will let it pass through me just like the moonlight. I will put it in your ears. I do not know what it will say to you. If you feel it split open your heart, put it on the paper and give it away. It is a gift from the moon and the earth and it is bigger than all of us. When you write it, I will learn. Maybe I will remember it in words. In my dog body, I do not tell you these things because my language is different. I speak in moves and smells. I speak by coming to you whenever you feel something. I just do not have the same needs, but I am reaching out just the same as you, trying to know more of all of us. Language doesn't stop us. It doesn't have to stop us. It's magic that we can talk together at all. This is magic that we have drawn by wanting to touch everything. That's what is around us now. That's what gives me this body that can talk in words. We made it together. I think I have silver hair because you want to see me as wise. If I touch my face right now, I know that it is smooth and accepting. It will give whatever picture anyone needs from it. We have been meeting like this, practicing this kind of storytelling for a long time. We are growing into it more and more. It is so much a part of us that it has slipped into our dog and our human forms. It comes in the daylight. It comes when we are quiet and can hear it. And it still draws us out into the moonlight where it is easy. The moon gives us comfort. She holds us while we practice making understandable language. This way we are not alone. We are more of everything. I cannot give you the memories of this. They are in you and around you. They are circling everything that you do. Maybe if you bleed into the earth you will leave a mark that you will find later."

    I smile because these are words that have come from somewhere else and we all know it. Thomas stands. He calls out, "Yes! Yes, I give myself to the knowing of all of this. I remember this circle in any way my spirit wishes. I feel everything. I feel so glad for this communion that I'm spilling out onto the earth right now."

    He takes a sticker and cuts his foot, and a few drops kiss the earth. I sigh.

p.s. They both go back into their beds and roll into their bodies until their breath is very deep. I lay under the tree waiting. Even outside I can hear her restlessness. I get up and I go into the shadows so I won't disturb her remembering.

Marilyn rolls out of bed and walks out into the night. She sees shadows all around except for the edge of the cliff. It is wondrously aglow. It calls to her. She walks out to the edge and turns back to face the mountain. The more she walks, the more she sees the moon start to pull up from the peak. At the edge of the cliff, she sees the moon balancing on the tip of the mountain. She fills with awe that it is still half full and hidden from the sight of some but not others. Marilyn waters the earth and gives thanks that she is awake to see it and then goes back to bed, wondering why she keeps waking up in the middle of the night.

p.p.s. I (Thomas) have a long cut on my left foot this morning that seems to have appeared without my remembering where it came from.

Forty

Today is bright and windy The sun is everywhere, but I can still see the moon. People have come to visit us. Hi, Anna. Hi, Lynn. Hi, Gary. Bali is down guarding the truck. Sniffing me. I understand.

Anna asks Thomas and Marilyn if they want to go up the mountain for a walk. Marilyn says, "Yes." I feel glad because I feel something deep in her body rise up and worship her spirit.

She needs to move and feel the wind and then the wind becomes the words and goes back into her body and back into her breath and finally into these stories. The words want to go through her body. They want to honor her humanness, as well. They are her spirit-walkers. The words are putting the memories where she can find them and where Thomas can hear them and where you can read them. In the daylight. Yes, a little walk will bring us some more stories.

Ogallalah de Oro

Thomas and I stay at the trailer so that Bali can run with her humans. I started up the path with them, but Thomas called me back. He likes me to be nearby. Even when he says he doesn't want me to watch after him. He says he doesn't need it. Then he keeps calling me to be close. So I sit with him and he sorts out his feelings while he works.

I lay by the Moqui stones. They are arranged in a circle like last night and I drift inside of them. Pretty soon, I am flying over the hills. I call out to the hikers when I see them. Marilyn has already started back down the mountain because she is ready for the story. She calls out to the others, "Look, look, it's a red-tailed hawk!"

I sigh and I drift back to the Moquis.

Forty One

"I feel the winds howling around my words."

So many things are happening. I feel the breaths getting shorter in my body. The rest of the lengths go out to the world and I do not follow them. I have to talk to you now.

There is a pushing on my belly, shouting out all my essence. Making me give it away. I am too old to birth puppies, so my belly births its wisdom. It is turning itself inside out and making my blood open to all.

How much of this you feel in your body, I do not know. My heart beats in my ears and I do not hear you the same. My body reaches for yours. They grasp each other to see what blood we have in common. It stretches me beyond my length. I know that it is a time of passage. Before I leave this body it seeks out the family to give away the very core of its passions and learnings. It bleeds away what has kept it alive deep inside. Take it. It will warm you through many winters. It will put the sun in your belly and cry wild.

Gather around. I offer you my deepest feelings because they are not mine. They have given birth to themselves. Now they are our children. Life spreads into more life. I am growing a new season so I share with you the harvest of this garden.

I listen to the earth. She spins faster and gives the circles to the stars. I feel new things of old times awakening in me. I know things that I have not seen before. I do not question them, but I am settled in awe. Every breath nourishes me in this wonder and I am amazed to see my body spin with the earth. My dreams have been many. I see when my eyes are closed and my body is asleep. The earth is beating with a new heart. It pounds faster and faster. We are both giving birth. I feel that she has watched this growing inside of her. She has picked this time to make more room in her family. She has put teachers on her surface to help all of us stretch and push out our newness with her. I feel her weep inside because it is her job. She feels all things, all beings. The earth knows every season and acts all of it out. Our bodies respond. Some of us act upon this, some do not.

This is what makes this a time of initiation. We are all moving deeper into the earth's belly and matching her. Our life with her life. For some, it is so close and so intimate it is scary. The fear comes to burn away our dead pieces.

My body is not afraid. It watches everything as it comes. I do not move faster than the seasons. I am a part of them. That is what I pass on to you. Here is the feeling of knowing your season and acting upon it. We all live in a time of passage. Everything is dying to make more life. If you feel the dying, then the next life comes to you and keeps you company during the passage.

    I feel the death inside of me and I feel it all around me, so I can walk with the next life, right now. I am not a remarkable being for this. I am part of a season. My cycle of life and death goes into the seasons. Then they are big enough for the whole world to receive.

    This initiation all around all of us trembles inside of me. I touch many tears that are still dry. I hear your screams that are still breathless. You have not impassioned this death because you are so afraid. You will not miss it. You will just give yourself more reasons to be afraid if you turn away from this now. I am an animal and I have given my choices to the earth, so I will cry for you and I will howl your name to the skies.

    Our time is now and everything in us must move aside for a new earth.

Forty Two

I hear you.

Some of you do not understand what I have said and others do not believe me. If I tell you all my truth, it is that the earth is dying and it must die before it puts on a new robe.

There, that's plain and you can look at it squarely or you can shut off your whole body and see nothing but the space inside of you. Either way, the vision is the same. Still, it is my vision and you may not understand it because you are birthing a different one.

So, I will tell you how I am living with what I see.

I am a guardian on this earth. I must feel all her cycles and I must act upon them. My body is dying. It is strong and kind and pushing. I am being propelled from deep inside of myself to everywhere else. I have been a very bright fire that is exploding and sending off sparks for any to see. I am not dying because I need to have sickness. I am dying because there is death in the air to feel and it is part of me. I do not turn my face away from the gifts my family offers. My belly matches the belly of the earth, I wear some of those rumblings. They do not tear me apart. They tear me away from keeping this body just because I want it to be mine.

All my life in this body I have guarded what belongs to me. I have watched over my food, my family, my feelings. I am quick to discipline those who touch without asking. I have come to learn the deepest attachments of all. Now I am in the initiation of this and the mother in my womb holds me and asks me to give away my life so that I can feel a greater life. Now I am giving away all of my possessions. I am offering up anything that I can cut from me. There are holes all over me and I will see what freedom gives me now.

I don't know what your initiation calls you to do, but I am discovering that mine has asked for my life. As I loosen my breath, I find all the winds joining me. My death is a prayer to all life.

I am not a guardian. This piece of death that is leaving me and going away, it goes to you (points to Brad.). It loves you. It touches all the death on your shoulders and it swirls into my belly and my legs. I shake it out my fur and there are sparks right into the sun. You are so hard and so strong. I see us just the same.

So I will thank us. And I will offer too that we are family and I know this inside of this body, right now. It is the season for those of us who feel the rites of passage. I am giving away the one that you have given to me and now it is passed on to all the others.

Forty Three

"My song to Thomas: We have been together because we are never apart. A long time inside of us we decided to be from the same heart. How could we not love each other? Meeting each other in different bodies and in different ways gives us more life and more love to share. Look for me. I come in forms you do not expect and that is a forever growing gift."

There. I found some poetry from my soul. It just appeared and it asked me to send it to you. It is your language becoming <u>our</u> language, more and more.

Hello Thomas. You know I haven't been one to talk much in this way. It has not been so simple or so easy for me [One word to me is a whole world to open, and I am careful.], but it has been natural for <u>you</u>. I watch the words from other hearts come to you. They are lots of different colors and shapes. You smile at them all. They go inside the top of your head and they shake and they breathe. Sooner or later you and Marilyn speak them. Amazing. Thank you. This is what I am learning from you.

You are being gifted by all these other beings, all kinds of them, in all kinds of places and times. You open a door and welcome them all. Then you have poetry and it's this poetry that goes to every heart and says, "Welcome."

I have been a guardian so well. I know how to dictate who comes to me and when and how. <u>And</u> I can change my "yes" to a "no" at any moment. I am in charge. I have the power of my destiny and my job running through me always.

You know I have given my guardianship to you. No matter what, I have always watched for you and around you. I haven't stopped you from doing anything[that's where you told me <u>you</u> were clearly in charge], but I am totally alert. Nothing changes that. I could never be too old, too sleepy, too sore to stop me from my appointed work.

I can tell you this-I love it. I love it just because it's there to love. You and I made up this life we share and this is my way to totally <u>live</u> it. I am utterly in it. I am utterly involved. I will never walk away from it, because it is deep inside me.

You are not feeling well today. I watched you through the night. Your stomach turns itself inside out-I know that feeling exactly. Do you know that you feel like this partly, because I am feeling like this, too?

I am dying. I told you that my spirit is gently turning my body inside out and emptying me to the winds. I am free every moment. It doesn't hurt me. Thank you for feeling this with me – you seem to be learning guardianship from my exposed core. Thank you and stop, if you want. I don't need you to come this way with me.

We are the same heart, but we do have different bodies.

My dogness jumps into this death. Everything I cared about is slipping away to the skies. What I am left with is the love....oh, and a new destiny to learn about. That's why we are finally talking like this and about this. I've emptied myself, so I can let others come to me, easily. I am learning, "Welcome." The more I say that, the more I find other ways to talk. To speak with spirit like you do, used to be too much for me. It was so strong and I had to stay so alert, even when I was asleep.

Part of me has been practicing this just by watching you. I am learning by being with you. I am sharing it as I can.

It's no wonder you feel my dying in your belly. We're family. We have birthed each other lots of times. This is easy for me. This is my natural gift. I don't know where it will take you.

Your body doesn't digest this, because you're afraid of my going[not a lot, but it seems to be enough to make you stop for a whole day and feel it]. You are human, and my jumping into these death cycles is the natural language-for me, not you. That's why you're learning it now. We always give each other our deepest, most sacred places.

If my gift feels like pain, I release you from it. Do you release you? If you must hurt, then I tell you that it is a way to be very alive together and to remember all our lives together. Pain burns a hole and inside of that you can see the next world and my new face.

Actually, you can see many faces around me, now. Our family is helping to make me ready and they're reminding you that there are others who want to live with you. Watch for a dog with a black face and a pink star, she will point you to a new life. She whispers to me that she has crow eyes; she looks from one, then the other ... there are lots of memories in the future......

    I want to tell all you others why I finally decided to speak at the end of my years,-it's time. You didn't need my words until now and I couldn't form them until your needs and desires said, "Welcome." There is a planet full of beings remembering their one heart now, and that is changing the heart. We can find each other in new places and we can talk like each other.

    Listen.

    I am just one part of the heart. There are others who specifically know <u>your</u> name. Find them. Together we are jumping into life and it will never be the same again.

    I am happy that you are patient enough to hear me. I am not always easy to know. I am a strong force who knows herself and I defend that because I must. If I have ever snapped at some of you, it's just our learning. It comes from love.

    Again, to Thomas, thank you, you have given me the heart to share myself here. Your blood has regenerated me so that I can be young in my old age. Your respect has given me comfort to learn new ways to be. Be patient, if you can, I am still learning.

Forty Four

To Marilyn – hello, hello, hello. It is simple and easy with us. I am not your guardian, so I can breathe slower with you. If I could laugh, I would laugh with you all the time.

You are silly. You change with the wind. I watch this. I do not understand it, but it excites me.

We have walked in your visions, but I have never told you this [maybe because I am just learning this now]. We are joined in the future. I am already slipping into a new body and you are holding me and whispering welcomes.

I saw you showing me who I will be. Like you, I will talk a lot and I will give away all the words. It is almost too astounding, but there it is, growing my belly. When I am new at my destiny, I invite you to laugh with me.

There are so many colors and beings around you.

Ogallalah de Oro

They protect you, so you don't need an earth guardian like me. I have enjoyed meeting all your clan. They are so easy to know, they have merged inside of me. They set free my cares.

    Thank you Thomas for being at the end of Hannah and at the beginning of Tundra.
    Thank you Marilyn for being at the end of Ogallalah and at the beginning of _____.

Afterwords

For him, it was a dream; after all, he was just a little boy. He was crying and he haltingly told me that he didn't believe that he was loved and that maybe he would never know love.......

So I took him in my arms and I rocked him. No words, we just matched the rhythm of the earth. When his grief was laid bare, he looked at me and asked who I was. I told him the truth. I told him I was one of the beings that loved him very much. I told him that I loved him so much that I would come and live with him one day.

Thomas' eyes widened, "Are you going to look like this?" he asked.

I had come as a lady all in white [he has seen me many times since then.]. He sensed that something as luminous as me couldn't possibly live side by side with him. Maybe he was right.

"No. I'll come however you wish. I can come as

a mother and take care of you, but I'll choose a body that you can understand." Then I smiled, and I melted into a black and white dog, big and wolf-like.

"Wow!" He was impressed. "Don't tell anybody. Please, huh? Don't tell anybody. I don't want them to make you go away."

"No. I promise I won't tell anybody until you're ready. I love you."

Thank you ~

Ogallalah's story weaves us into all other lives, and we are honored, deeply, that you are a part of that. We invite you to connect with us even more. Tell us how these words have entered your heart.

Share this with others if you wish. Let bookstores know that you want to see Ogallalah de Oro on their shelves. That's how unusual, magical stories find their way to lots of hearts – we all have to ask for them. We have to ask to hear the words that speak the ancient and new earth languages.

Let us know if we can help. We travel all over the country doing: spirit storytellings, booksignings, gatherings, rituals, private readings, and probably anything you feel moved to ask.

Twintreess
TreeHouse Press
5738 E. Holmes Street
Tucson, AZ 85711 USA
Phone: 520-750-9755

Other titles by Twintreess:
The Heart of Matter
Etheric Songs from the Children of Earth
naturespeak
Meditations on Regeneration

Just call or write us at the above address for a catalog. Thanks.